SPECIAL MESSAGE TO READERS

JUNGLE FEVER

Eager to climb out from under the shadow of her famous mother, Eva manages to secure a place on a scientific expedition to the Amazon, determined to prove her own worth. But her steamy surroundings quickly build up heat of a different nature, as she finds herself increasingly attracted to the eminently desirable Dan. Then two surprise additions to the expedition turn everything upside-down. Will jealousies, family strife, and the deadly dangers of the tropics get in the way of Eva and Dan's future happiness?

CAROL MacLEAN

JUNGLE
FEVER

Complete and Unabridged

LINFORD
Leicester

First published in Great Britain in 2013

First Linford Edition
published 2014

A catalogue record for this book is available
from the British Library.

ISBN 978–1–4448–2155–0

Published by
F. A. Thorpe (Publishing)
Anstey, Leicestershire

Set by Words & Graphics Ltd.
Anstey, Leicestershire
Printed and bound in Great Britain by
T. J. International Ltd., Padstow, Cornwall

This book is printed on acid-free paper

1

Eva Martinez bit down on her finger-nail. Her thick, black hair was caught up in a careless twist, sweeping it away from her face, but tendrils had escaped. She was wearing her one good skirt, but the hem hung down in one part. Eva noticed none of this. Inside her head, only one thought was beating. *He had to let her go. He had to let her go.* She was the last candidate. There had been at least ten people in the university library when she arrived. One by one they had been called into Professor Grierson's office and after half an hour or so of interview, reappeared.

Eva had studied their faces, trying to discover whether they'd been accepted or rejected. It was hard to say. She knew a couple of them vaguely, from her time as a research student in the zoology department at Kent University. They had both followed research contracts here to London West so she wasn't surprised to see them. Daisy Kew for example, who specialised in tropical finches. Daisy was a naturally happy person, so her wide smile as she left the Professor's office meant nothing. Greg Smith was born with a poker face so she learnt very little from his expression as he brushed past her on his way out. Greg wasn't blessed with social skills and she hoped he hadn't joined the expedition. A month in his company, in a small jungle campsite, would be a trial.

Now she was alone and waiting. She heard the professor cough and the creak of his chair through the half-open door to his office, but she couldn't quite see him or what he was doing. How long was he going to keep her waiting? She'd been so keen this morning that she'd arrived an hour before her appointment time, determined to show him her mettle and suitability for the project. Just then, the door swung open. Eva leapt to her feet, excited and nervous. This was her chance! She had taken one step in the direction of the door when a large man strode through the library and straight into the professor's office, ignoring her squeak of protest. She had an impression of his hair, as thick and black as her own, a tanned face wearing a dark scowl and a powerful breadth of shoulders as he went by. She sat on the edge of her chair, both annoyed and curious about this sudden turn of events.

The man had forgotten to shut the door after him and Eva listened in unashamedly. After all, it was meant to be her in there right at that moment. He'd stolen her slot.

'Ah, Dan, I thought you might turn up. Take a seat, there's a good chap.' Professor Grierson's booming voice penetrated the air.

'Damn it, Bob! What do you mean by leaving me a voicemail telling me I can't go on the expedition? It's outrageous. You know you need me.

What are you playing at?'

Whoever Dan was, he had a voice which suited him, Eva decided, leaning forward precariously to hear more. It was deep and gritty and very angry, and for some reason made the little hairs on the back of her neck raise up.

'I don't think I quite said that, did I?' The professor sounded vague and faintly surprised. 'No, what I said, or meant, was that I was fully expecting *both* you and Rose to be coming along on my little expedition. Now I find that although I have a trip doctor, I'm missing my expert linguist. And all because you've decided not to be a gentleman and marry the girl.'

'Who told you the wedding was off?' Dan sounded coldly furious.

'Rose told me herself. Came here in floods of tears yesterday. You really have treated her appallingly, my dear chap. Jilted two days before her marriage. Terrible.' But the Professor was vague, as if mouthing what was right and proper. Eva imagined he was still mulling over where he'd find a replacement linguist.

'I'm glad that I picked your message up wrongly. After all, how would you get another expedition doctor at such short notice?' Dan asked. 'One who's had all the necessary immunisations and has tropical disease expertise? I doubt very much that you could.' His tone was confident to the point of arrogance, Eva thought. She felt a little sorry for the professor until she remembered she was going to have to persuade him to take her on. Hopefully Dan would pave the way with his bullying manner. Poor Rose, getting dumped by him just before the wedding. What a horrible thing to do to one's fiancée. She added Dan to the list with Greg Smith on it. Two people she prayed wouldn't be going to Trinita Island.

'Oh I dare say I'd manage something,' Professor Grierson said mildly. 'Thing is, I'd rather like you to speak to Rose. Try and persuade her to change her mind. She doesn't need to be married to you to join the expedition.'

'Rose has made it very clear that she'll only go if we get married as we were supposed to.' Dan's voice was clipped to a sharp edge. 'That's not happening. So I suggest if you want Rose on the trip then you speak to her yourself.'

The Professor mumbled something which Eva couldn't catch. Then there was a sound of him clearing his throat. 'Now, dear fellow, was there anything else? Only, I've one more student to interview today. And lunchtime is looming.'

There was a bellow of suppressed rage and Dan stormed out of the room. His dark face was thunderous and he brushed past Eva without acknowledging her. Very like Greg, then. Only much, much better looking. He had unusual tawny eyes under black brows, a classical Roman nose and carved lips. There was a hint of a cleft in his chin and his jaw was strong. He was tall, at least six-foot-two, and lean. She felt a shaft of pure physical attraction.

'Miss Martinez?'

She went into the office, having completely forgotten her rehearsed introduction and résumé. All she could think of was long, powerfully muscled legs striding past her and the faintest scent of male spice.

'Martinez,' the professor repeated, then knocked himself gently on the forehead in memory. 'Ah yes, Gwendolin's daughter.'

Eva bit back a retort. For once, it would be wonderful to simply be her. But as usual, her mother's reputation cast a long shadow under which Eva seemed destined to live up to her entire life. 'Yes, I'm Professor Martinez's daughter,' she said.

The professor nodded, relaxing back into his leather armchair. His wild mane of white hair stood up as if he'd had a shock, and his eyes were astonishingly blue and clear for a man in his mid-seventies. He looked at her assessingly. 'Have you been to the tropics before?' he asked bluntly.

Eva felt at a disadvantage. Her prepared speech, full of her previous experience and transferable skills, had come back to her but were no help when faced with a direct question like that. 'Not the tropics, no,' she hedged, 'but I have travelled a lot generally. I spent my childhood flying between London and New York and recently I've carried out research projects in Wales and Scotland.'

'What is your subject, remind me?' he asked, not unkindly. He flicked through her résumé papers as she answered.

'Animal behaviour, with a focus on amphibians. I want to work with poison arrow frogs in Trinita. No one's ever studied them there and I know there's a special cave-dwelling population which is highly unusual. I — '

'It says here you're still writing up your PhD,' he interrupted her.

'Yes, that's right. I got a little bit behind on it. But I've been doing some post-grad research, as I said, and — '

Professor Grierson shook his head gently. 'I'm taking experienced scientists along on this trip. It clearly stated that on the application form. The fact you haven't finished your PhD tells me you have some work to do. I'm very sorry, Eva, to have to say no. Especially as I have the utmost respect for your mother. She really is a wonderful scientist. No, I can't take you.' He rose to escort her out.

'I'll work for no pay,' she said desperately, not budging from his office.

'You can't persuade me, although as Gwendolin's daughter I have every confidence that you know your subject,' the professor told her, taking her elbow and guiding her to the door. 'Now you need to prove that by finishing your doctorate and passing your viva and getting it published. A tall order by the end of the month, which is when we leave,' he finished with heavy humour.

'What if I could get a reference?' Eva

asked quickly, before he could shut the door on her. 'Someone to sponsor me?'

Bob Grierson scratched his head. 'Possibly. But I don't see how that can make up for your lack of field experience.'

Eva stumbled down the steps of the sandstone building, holding back angry tears. She couldn't believe it. She'd blown her chance. For years her mother had been telling her what a brilliant man the professor was and how he only took on the best crop of students and post-graduates to work with him. How they thrived under his tutelage and went on to better contracts and even tenure in top universities or well-paying jobs in industry. She'd lapped it all up, promising herself that she would be one of them and make her mother proud of her. The opportunity to go to the South American island of Trinita had been a dream come true when she saw the circulated email and flyer going round the university in Kent. She was finishing her current studies and needed a next step to move onto. A month describing new amphibian species on an unstudied tropical island would set her apart from the competition and hopefully get her a contract in London. It would be good to be back in her home city.

Now the whole summer lay ahead, blank of promise. She pulled her hair back savagely into a high knot and adjusted her uncomfortable skirt. She wasn't used to heels either, and the sides of her shoes were digging into her toes. Beyond was the engine noise of the city, the shouts of its citizens and the taste of its fumes and grime. She left the university grounds and went across a busy road to a row of shops, jumbled together selling eclectic goods such as antiques, secondhand clothes and African vegetables. There was a tiny coffee shop squeezed in between 'Gambia Goods' and 'Elleswood Road Antiques'. A coffee would be good — large, black and bitter, like her mood.

An old-fashioned bell chimed as she went in. It was gloomy inside and crammed with cane wood tables and spindly cane stools. There was one other customer, a man sitting in the darkest corner with a tall latte in front of him which was untouched. Eva went straight to the tiny counter and asked for a coffee and a baklava dripping in honey, from the selection. The old lady nodded and indicated she would bring it over. Her accent was strongly eastern European, making the café seem exotic and special.

Eva turned to choose a table and stopped with a jolt. The man sitting brooding at the table, not sipping his drink, was Dan. She had a sudden moment of complete clarity. A solution to her problem that was blinding in its brilliance. Without hesitating, Eva went over to him. 'Hello, do you mind if I join you?'

Dan looked pointedly at the several empty tables. While he did so, Eva slipped onto the stool opposite. The old lady smiled as she laid out carefully a china cup of aromatic coffee and a flower-patterned plate with an oozing slice of baklava on it, moving the latte to make way for Eva's selection. Dan looked bemused. A slight twitch of his lips indicated an appreciation of the scene but vanished once the owner had gone.

'Do I know you?' he enquired coolly.

'You don't know me but you've seen me before,' Eva countered. She bit into the baklava, releasing a slow gloop of honey which dribbled onto her chin.

'You must have an incredibly sweet tooth to eat that,' he said. Again, a hint of amusement.

'Do I detect a note of disapproval?' she asked, wiping her chin with the paper napkin provided. 'You should have some, it's delicious.'

Dan shook his head as though to clear cobwebs. 'Can we start again? Have I seen you before? Because I don't remember you.'

Eva couldn't help but feel disappointed. She had made no impression

13

on this man in the few minutes they had passed each other. Yet he had imprinted on her mind and skin like a burning brand. She felt a tingling awareness of him, a heightened tension of her skin as if it would draw her across the table to touch him. With chagrin, she tried to be as cool and off-hand as him. 'You were in Professor Grierson's office. Talking to him about his expedition to Trinita?'

'You're the student who was waiting.'

'That's right.' She paused. 'I couldn't help overhearing your conversation. It sounds like we can help each other.'

'Can we indeed, Miss — ?' Dan looked her up and down lazily.

Eva shivered under his amber gaze. Her skin prickled as if he'd reached out to caress her instead of simply looking. 'Martinez, Eva Martinez.' She introduced herself belatedly and waited for the inevitable query about her mother. It didn't come. Instead he took a long sip of the latte and set the cup down. 'Did you hear my offer?' she persisted.

'What exactly are you offering, Miss Eva Martinez?' The tone was low and honeyed, playful like a jungle tiger.

Eva flushed. This wasn't going the way she'd imagined in her flash of insight. He was meant to be grateful to her and agreeable instantly to her suggestion. 'I'll cut straight to it then,' she said, wishing her voice wasn't so breathless. 'I want to go on Professor Grierson's expedition to Trinita, and you owe him a linguist, if this Rose isn't going. I'm fluent in Spanish, which is the main language on the island.'

There was a moment of utter silence in the café. Then his laughter rang out loud and harshly.

'What's so funny? Can't you see it's perfect?' Her voice rose with annoyance.

'You've got pluck, I'll admit that.' Dan leaned back on his chair, looking at her intently. 'But I don't owe the professor anything. So I don't need you.'

'He seems very keen that your

. . . fiancée Rose goes with you. And if she won't, from what you say, then he still needs a translator. And that's me.'

'Ex-fiancée,' Dan said. 'Why do you need me for this? Why not speak directly to the professor?'

'Because I can't go back to him without a reference from a sponsor. And I'm hoping that you're going to write it,' Eva said, with more buoyancy than she felt. Her impulsive idea was beginning to feel distinctly shaky. But Professor Grierson hadn't said an outright 'no' when she'd asked about mentoring. *Possibly*, he'd said. A word with at least some promise. She might not have enough field experience in her scientific studies, but he hadn't said anything about her other skills.

'You've thought it all through, haven't you? I admire your cold logic. Women always know how to get what they want, don't they?'

'I need an answer,' she said, ignoring the note of bitterness in his voice. What was his problem, anyway? Hadn't he just jilted poor Rose, whoever she was, rather than the other way around? If anyone was demonstrating cold logic and getting what they wanted, it was him!

'I need to be on Bob's expedition. Trinita is the only know location for Harrap virus, which affects the local indigenous people, and Bob's the only outsider who has links with the local chiefs and can get me into the villages. I'm not sure your command of Spanish will be of any use there — they speak local dialects.'

'And finding the cause of the disease will make your name,' Eva guessed, ignoring his last words.

'I was thinking more of finding a cure,' he said wryly. 'Have you seen the symptoms?'

Eva blushed. He wasn't quite the hard-headed ambitious doctor she'd portrayed with her comment. Dan drummed his fingers on the table top. They were nice fingers, she noted — long and tapered with neat, clean nails. They looked strong and capable, like the rest of him. She glanced up to find his gold-flecked eyes unsettlingly fixed on her. She stared back boldly.

'Okay, you've got a deal,' he said, 'I'll write your reference and speak to Bob on your behalf, Miss Martinez.'

The bell chimed and a girl came in and ordered a cappuccino. She stared at Dan and Eva and a slow smile spread across her face. Dan acknowledged her with a nod of his head. Eva wondered why she looked so intrigued. As she watched, the girl put a lid on her takeaway coffee and hurried out the door. By the time she passed the window she was talking on her mobile animatedly.

Eva let herself into the tall house off Sloane Square. Her feet sank into deep pile carpet, muffling her entrance. The hall smelled of lavender wax and a light flowered fragrance which the house-keeper sprayed into the air each day. The house was elegantly furnished with tasteful antique furniture and many valuable ornaments, a testament to her mother's success in life. The irony of it was that her father's New York apartment was equally furnished with good taste and wealth. They had so much in common, and yet couldn't find common ground on which to live together.

'Is that you, Eva?' Gwendolin called from somewhere in the vast chamber of the ground floor to the front of the house. Eva dropped her handbag onto the nearest fragile Queen Anne chair and kicked off her shoes with a sigh of relief. She padded through to the room Gwendolin used as her day office. Her mother was bent over some notes, writing on the paper in red ink in her spiky, agitated style. Her ash-blonde hair glinted with summer sunshine from the large window at the desk. Eva had taken after her father in colouring, inheriting only her height and slimness from her mother.

'Mother, I'm going to South America,' she said.

'Don't call me that. I have a given

19

name which as you know I much prefer.' Her back remained bent and feverish with the flourish of each absorbed pen stroke.

'Very well, *Gwendolin*, I'm leaving the country.'

'Congratulations. Travelling with that young red-headed creature you brought home last month, I suppose?'

'Not Gavin,' Eva said. It hadn't been a serious affair. He was a friend, that was all. How typical of Gwendolin to congratulate her without being shocked or intrigued or curious.

'Aren't you the least bit interested in how and why?' she asked, piqued.

'It's your life.' Gwendolin had finally turned from her marking to look at her daughter. The tip of the pen tapping gently on her upper lip suggested her mind wasn't entirely concentrated on Eva. 'You've always been foolhardy and impetuous. You take after your father. You'll wake up in the morning and regret it, but then you can change your mind.' She raised a finger as if she'd remembered something and bent back to her paper to write it down.

Eva clenched her fists, keeping her arms dangling straight at her sides. She shouldn't let Gwendolin rile her. All she wanted was her approval. Some sign that she met with Gwendolin's appreciation.

'I'm going on an expedition. I've met someone who's going to support my application. He's called Dan. Dan . . .' she realised she didn't even know his surname. All she had was his mobile number and a promise to call to arrange details.

'Let's talk about it later, sweetie. I have twenty exam papers to mark before tomorrow. Honestly, I wonder whether they teach spelling and grammar anymore.'

Eva woke at three o'clock in the morning with a quiver of fear. What was she doing? She was rushing headlong into a journey to South America on the flimsy premise of using her Spanish, and in reality wanting to carry out her scientific research once there. Not only that, but she'd persuaded a total stranger to be her sponsor in order to get there. She sat up in bed. Around her the night noises continued. London never slept. There were always cars driving somewhere, taxis hooting, and the low buzz of an overcrowded city which hung like a pall everywhere. It was comforting. She'd forgotten how much she loved it. She got out of bed and pulled back the curtain. The street was tree-lined and the leaves were rippling in a breeze outside. A small brown moth battered itself against the glass pane, trying to get in. She remembered pictures in a book about South America which showed huge colourful butterflies as big as birds.

A flare of excitement coursed through her. She was going to take Professor Grierson at his word. She would turn up at the airport at the end of the month with her glowing reference and her perfect Spanish and she would travel to Trinita. She tried not to think of the fact that she had never travelled so far and to such an exotic location before. An image conjured up of Dan by her side on the trip made her heart thump strangely faster.

2

Dan wore a sombre suit for the pre-expedition slide night and party. Eva was late and he wondered briefly whether she'd got cold feet and decided not to go through with the whole thing. He wouldn't blame her if she had, but perversely he was disappointed. Although the whole thing was a farce, he was committed to doing it. They'd spoken only twice in the weeks leading up to this, by phone, and then only to arrange details such as her confirmation of her Spanish qualifications and fluency. She'd sent him her research record, too, and details of her doctorate.

Unfortunately, Rose's betrayal had left him suspicious and untrusting of any woman. If Dan was honest with himself, and he usually tried to be, there was more than one reason for agreeing to sponsor Eva. Yes, he wanted to be in Bob's good books by providing a translator, since Rose was no longer available. He was determined to get to Trinita and talk to the villagers. He wanted to investigate the endemic disease there. But there was more than a hint of revenge in what he was doing. Rose's affair with his best friend while they were engaged had cut him to the core. His heart was wounded beyond repair. Let her see that he'd found someone else to replace her immediately. She needn't know the true nature of his relationship with Eva. She'd find out soon enough through the grapevine that Dan had been seen with another woman. Her friend had seen them together in the coffee shop. He intended to play on that. Let her see that his life would, and could, go on without her. Even if it was all window-dressing. He'd never love again. He wouldn't let someone else in so close.

'Don't worry, she'll turn up,' Daisy Kew said, touching his arm lightly.

Daisy and her husband Sam were both going on the expedition. Dan had known them both for years and they were good friends. They were the only ones he'd told about Rose and what had truly happened between them. Everyone else believed Rose's version of the truth. He could tell Daisy didn't like what he was doing today but was too kind to say it. He looked at her open, smiling face and wondered why he couldn't fall for a woman like her — uncomplicated, warm and without wiles.

'Does Bob know you're going to be Eva's sponsor?' Daisy asked.

'No. He'll find out tonight,' Dan said.

The music swelled and someone called out that the bar was open. As ever, the party had been gate-crashed by many students and staff completely unlinked to Bob's Trinita trip. Everyone enjoyed a free drink.

'How are your parents and Tom?' Daisy asked. She didn't need to spell out to Dan what she meant.

'Still in shock. I'm *persona non grata* right now.' He hadn't told them the whole story.

They were so sad over his split from Rose. His older brother Tom was happily married and totally in love with Marianne, with twin babies on the way. His parents were still in love and showed it unashamedly every day. No, they weren't happy with him, but he wasn't ready to reveal the depths to which Rose had sunk. It would only shock and disgust them more.

'I just want this out of the way,' he added. 'I'd like to get on with packing for the trip. There's a lot to organise.'

Daisy nodded over to the door. 'Here she comes. It's not too late to back out, Dan. You hardly know her, so why do you have to sponsor her? What if she lets you down? I can get Sam to go and tell her.'

Dan glanced over to where Daisy indicated. Eva stood there, looking uncertain, dressed in a crimson summer dress. He was struck again by her looks. She wasn't

pretty — her cheekbones were too pro-
nounced and her mouth over-large — but
she was striking. Her raven hair con-
trasted with her pale skin and grey eyes.
Without wanting it, a pulse of desire
shot through him. He was annoyed by
it. It was the last thing he needed, like a
needle plunged into his skin. He frowned,
and at the same time she noticed him.
Her shoulders went back and she stood
straight and slender with a determined
expression as if bristling for battle. In a
different place it would've amused him.
Then he realised he was still frowning
and she must've thought he was frowning at her. He forced a polite smile and
she relaxed and walked towards him.

Eva gripped her handbag tightly. Dan
was staring at her as if he hated her.
When he saw her catching his expression he'd masked it with a smile. What
did that mean? Perhaps he blamed her,
rightly, for the odd piece of theatre they
found themselves acting out today. But
he was a grown man and he'd entered
into the agreement, knowing what he

was doing. She felt that inexorable pull towards him, an almost physical tug like two cores of gravity drawn together. Or probably it was only on her side. He showed no sign of liking her, let alone being attracted to her. It was better that way, she decided. She wanted to concentrate on her studies in Trinita without distraction. She was determined to be the best of Professor Grierson's students, making her mother proud and helping her get a good research contract after the summer.

'Let's get this over with as painlessly as possible,' Dan said as she approached.

'Said like a true doctor,' she replied lightly. It was silly to feel hurt by his words. Didn't she, too, want it over with quickly and matter-of-factly, so she could plan for the expedition?

'You know Daisy and Sam?' Dan went on.

Eva smiled at Daisy and was introduced to Sam, a bear of a man, the very image of a Viking, but with a gentleness that matched Daisy's. She caught Daisy's glance at her dress.

'I wasn't sure how formal tonight was, so I hedged my bets with this. I borrowed it from a friend.' *Stop it, Eva. Stop gabbling. Don't show your nerves.*

'Actually I was admiring the colour. It's perfect for you, and such a happy shade,' Daisy said nicely.

Professor Grierson was standing at the other end of the room, staring at a laptop and talking to a technician who was kneeling on the floor with a scart cable. At Dan and Eva's approach he swung round and raised his eyebrows. There was an air of unreality and it felt to Eva as if she couldn't draw enough breath to fill her lungs. Yet despite her nervousness, she felt suddenly alive with anticipation. This was her key to Trinita and to adventure.

'Bob.' Dan nodded. 'You've met Eva Martinez?'

'Miss Martinez, yes of course. An unexpected pleasure to see you again.' There was a question in his pleasant greeting.

The technician stood up triumphantly and Eva had a second to compose herself as he turned on the laptop and the Powerpoint presentation lit up the wall screen.

'So, what's this about, Dan?' Bob Grierson asked.

Eva stilled as Dan explained his sponsorship of her. He kept it short and concise and she was impressed by his cool confidence once again. Then she held her breath while they waited for the professor's response. He tapped away at the laptop, then gave them a brief nod. 'Very well. If Dan thinks you're up to it, then I'm happy to have you on the team. We need a Spanish speaker at the very least. If you're as good as Dan says you are, then you'll pick up the local lingo quickly too.' He turned back to the laptop but Eva wasn't finished.

Before she could think it through, she blurted out, 'I'd like to study the frog populations too. I can do that and be ready to translate when needed.'

She was ready for his booming voice to argue and dismiss her. But he chuckled. 'You're a determined young lady. I can see that. Very well. We'll see you at the airport at the end of the month.'

Yes! She'd done it. She walked away quickly in case he changed his mind, following Dan back to where Daisy and Sam were chatting with other friends.

'The others can't make it tonight,' Daisy was saying. 'There's a divers' conference on at Sussex Uni that they've gone to and I think James and Christa must still be up in Scotland.'

Eva was secretly relieved. It would be too overwhelming meeting everybody in one go. It was nice to meet Daisy and Sam in advance. At least she'd know them when she reached the airport. And Dan. She glanced at him. His face was brooding and he kept looking over at the door as if expecting someone. A girl, vivacious in a lilac silk tunic and white leggings, said something to him and laughed, inviting him into the group. Eva felt apart. Then the door opened and her mother walked in. The lights dimmed and the professor asked everyone to sit as his presentation was about to start.

★   ★   ★

Gwendolin grabbed Eva at the interval as she made an excuse to find the cloakrooms. Dan was still in conversation with his friends and Eva had to have a moment to herself to adjust to what she'd done. But it wasn't to be; her mother was too fast.

'I don't like the look of him. What were you thinking of? He looks . . . dangerous.'

'That's a ridiculous thing to say. You haven't even met Dan properly yet.'

'What do you know about him? It's awfully sudden, isn't it, this trip, this sponsorship? I'm sure you can't have known him long.' Gwendolin took off her hat and smoothed the feathers on it into shape.

'How would you know? You wouldn't notice if I brought Brad Pitt home. Besides, I don't need to know him well. All I need from him is a reference and sponsorship to travel to Trinita.'

'That really is a silly comment. Of course I notice what you're doing. I'm your mother. That's why I'm warning you about Dan and running off to South America. Are you sure about this? Really sure?'

'It's a bit late now for discussion. In case it hasn't sunk in, I've bought my plane tickets and I'm going!' Eva's anger soared. When had Gwendolin ever taken a true interest in what her daughter was up to? Her whole life was about jumping up and down to get noticed by her parents. No wonder she did daft, impulsive things. There was no one to stop her or advise her.

'There's no need to be like that,' Gwendolin said sharply, 'I can see when I'm not wanted. I have to go in any case; I've a lecture to give.'

Eva sighed as her mother walked

away, her body rigid with indignation. At the door she almost collided with a girl coming in. Then, with a shake of her feathered hat, she was gone. The girl was petite with long, silky, straight blonde hair and big, blue eyes that were made baby blue by her pale blue suit. Those eyes were welling with unshed tears and Eva looked on in fascinated horror as she loudly burst in to wails and let the tears pour down her perfect delicate face.

'Rose! What on earth are you doing here?' Dan said.

'Oh Dan. Please, please tell me it isn't true,' Rose wept prettily. 'Tell me you aren't seeing someone else. I love you so much. It can't be true. It can't be.'

Why did Dan move to Eva's side? She frowned at him. What was this all about?

'I thought . . . I hoped we could try again. We were meant to be together.' Rose clasped her hands together, looking frail and sweetly vulnerable. Only the hardest heart could rebuff her, Eva thought.

'You're too late,' Dan said brutally. 'I've moved on with my life, Rose. You should too.'

Rose turned to Eva and shot her a glance of pure malice. It made Eva take a step back. What was Rose thinking? That she and Dan were together? She started to deny it but Rose was speaking passionately, her gaze fixed purely on Dan.

'Darling, it doesn't matter. We can work it out together. It's not impossible. I don't care about her. You know you love me more than you'll ever love this person or anyone else. You know it, Dan!' Rose spoke with breathy passion directly to him. There might have been no one else in the room.

'Please leave quietly, Rose. If not, I'll have to ask Sam to escort you out.' Dan turned deliberately from her, taking Eva with him.

She pulled free angrily. He was the most horrible man imaginable. How could he be so awful to Rose, especially after dumping her? She must love him so much to beg for him to take her back even after his appalling behaviour. And Eva was certainly not going to be party to his heartlessness by linking arms and acting as if they were an . . . *item*!

With another great sob, Rose flung herself at the door and ran away. There was a silence in the room. Then Daisy was gathering up drinks orders and chatting brightly to fill the gap. Sam looked uncomfortable and Dan was wearing a black scowl.

'I've got to go,' Eva said, which wasn't entirely true. When visualising this evening she'd imagined that she and Dan could get acquainted. But after the scene with Rose, she'd changed her mind. She had no intention of getting to know him better now or in the future. He was a cold, monstrous man if he couldn't be melted by Rose's pleas. A man who could jilt his intended bride two days before their wedding wasn't a good person, full stop. Dan Adams had proved that.

'What a shame,' Daisy said, sounding embarrassed on her and Dan's behalf.

'We'll see you at the airport, then?' She nudged Dan, who was glaring at the ground, unseeing.

'I'll be in touch,' he said shortly.

'Don't bother,' Eva replied, in an equally short tone. 'I don't need anything from you. Just your signature on my references.' She swung on her heel and missed Dan's wince.

* * *

Eva sat on top of her suitcase and tried to squash it shut. A T-shirt had escaped out of one side, while one leg of a pair of tropical khaki trousers was dancing out of the other. She managed finally to get the clasp fastened. Her room was full of equipment and bags of clothes, medicines and maps and books for the expedition. She could hardly believe she was going the next day. The ring of her mobile phone reminded her of Dan. He'd called on her mobile three times since the party the evening before. She'd let it go to voicemail. He couldn't possibly have anything to say that she needed to hear. She deleted the messages without listening to them. He couldn't justify his behaviour towards Rose and even if he was phoning to apologise, she wasn't interested. The less she had to do with Dan, the better.

An uneasy little thought about sharing space in a small campsite wormed its way into her mind. She shut it down. She had no idea about jungle expeditions, but perhaps they would all share a big, communal tent or camp out under the stars. She wasn't going to worry about Dan's proximity. She was going to study her taxonomy books and prepare for her research project. But she couldn't help licking her lip with the tip of her tongue at the memory of his arm pressed on hers and the shockwave that had passed through her body at his touch.

3

Eva was almost sick with the excitement of getting to the airport, combined with the shockingly early rise in the morning. She wove her way through a throng of holiday-makers in the airport check-in queues, her unwieldy suitcase screeching on its casters while its matching shoulder-bag banged against her hip with each stride. She tried to spot Professor Grierson's white hair.

There it was, like a beacon, ahead. Around him was a small group of people. She glimpsed Daisy and Sam and then Dan, standing out from the others by his height, looking impossibly gorgeous in a tropical shirt and tan trousers, a canvas bag slung over his shoulder. There it was, that sharp punch to the chest when she saw him. It had to stop. Thinking of his behaviour to Rose was like a dousing of ice water. She wanted nothing to do with him, she told herself. The group began to move in the direction of the nearest gate.

She speeded up, but the casters failed and her suitcase veered off, crashing to the ground and springing open. All sorts of items freed themselves and spread out on the shiny floor. She crouched down and tried to gather them up. Her shoulder-bag slew round and banged into her painfully before joining the larger case on the ground.

'Can I help?' Dan hunkered down beside her.

'I can manage, thank you.' Eva snatched up a lacy pink bra and flushed as Dan grinned.

Annoyingly, he ignored her put-down and began to pick up her stuff and replace it in the suitcase. 'You're not going on a package holiday. This luggage is totally unsuitable for where we're going,' he said, shaking his head and making Eva bristle at his patronising tone. 'Didn't you get my messages?'

41

'What messages?' She wasn't going to admit to deleting them. With embarrassment she realised they weren't apologies for the party after all.

'I left you instructions for what to bring.'

'On whose authority, might I ask?' Eva said snappily. What an arrogant man! What right did he have to tell her what to do?

'Bob asked me to keep you right. But having ignored my calls, you've brought the wrong cases. You can't carry these into the thick of the jungle.'

'Well, if I'd known that's what you were calling about, I'd have listened,' she said, dragging the handle of the suitcase up.

'What did you think I was calling about?' He was laughing at her, Eva was sure. The giveaway twitch of his mouth irritated her.

'I'm ready,' she said abruptly, spinning on her heel to get to the gate that the others had already disappeared into.

'Not so fast.' Dan caught hold of her arm.

A bolt of electricity shot along her veins at his touch. Angrily, she shook him off. She didn't want it and she didn't want him. Why couldn't her body understand that?

'Eva, be sensible. I'll take you to the travel shop. There should be just enough time to get you kitted out before the gate closes. Now hurry.' Dan spoke sharply with a command in his voice she couldn't ignore.

Fuming silently, she followed his tall figure to the shop, noticing the admiring glances he was getting from other women. If they knew what he was really like, they wouldn't bother, she thought childishly. At least he hadn't commented on her clothes. Her hiking boots, cotton jeans and chequered blouse must have passed his test. She'd tied a bandanna into her thick curls in an attempt to keep her hair out of her eyes and she carried a rain jacket, since she'd vaguely heard that the rainy season started in July in Trinita. In the shop, Dan was swift and competent, buying a large, waterproof rucksack and small day kitbag for her. A plastic water bottle and small medicine pouch were added and at the last moment he put a compass on the counter too.

'Unless you brought one?' he queried.

She shook her head, still too annoyed at his bossiness to speak.

Once they'd left the shop, he quickly repacked her belongings with quiet efficiency until the loudspeaker announced the gate closure for Venezuelan flights. Then they were both running along the corridor, leaving Eva's empty suitcase lying open and abandoned. Dan carried her new rucksack with ease. Reluctantly she admitted to herself that he'd done a good job of kitting her out. But she wouldn't be beholden to him. As they reached the row of plastic chairs where the others were still waiting to board, she paused for breath. 'I'll pay you back once I find my purse,' Eva said.

'Don't worry about it. I can't have my sponsored student letting me down with her equipment,' Dan mocked.

It came as a shock, the reminder of her need to succeed. Somehow Eva had managed to forget the tie between them. She sat down just as the call came to board. Above the corridor leading to the plane was a digital board reading 'Trinita'. Eva forgot about everything else in a leap of anticipation. The adventure was finally beginning.

*   *   *

She was unprepared for the wall of damp heat that hit them when they left the air-conditioned airport at Galanga. It was like stuffing a wet sock into her mouth to breathe. She had a sudden panic that she couldn't bear it, but after a few minutes it was easier and she found her breath. Bob Grierson had organised a minibus to take them from the main town of Galanga up into the northern jungle. Eva was pleased that her Spanish was invaluable when the bus driver began to haggle over the price of the bus rental. Bob Grierson had shrugged helplessly when the man began a torrent of language. She negotiated a deal to the satisfaction of both parties and flushed in delight at Bob's gruff thanks.

She squashed in with the others into the old bus, wishing Dan wasn't right next to her. She felt the hard strength of his leg pressing against hers in the crowded space. On the other side she had Daisy, who was trying not to push against her too.

'Sorry, Eva, I'm digging my elbow into your side. If Sam wasn't taking up more than his fair share of space it'd be a lot better.'

There was a squawk of indignation from Sam, quickly smothered by a kiss from Daisy.

Eva looked at the people who would be her companions for the next two months. Daisy had done a round of introductions during the plane journey. Apart from Bob Grierson, Daisy, Sam and Dan, there were three other couples. Anne and Brian Scopes were marine biologists and scuba divers who'd be spending their time surveying the coral reefs off the coast. They were both thin and intense, with greying hair, as if they'd grown to look alike over the years of their marriage. Christa and James Leven were a Scottish couple who were going to be recording butterfly species in the jungle canopy. James was a caricature of a Scotsman, with ruddy cheeks and flaming red hair, while Christa was brown-haired with more than her fair share of freckles. They were both climbers, they had told Eva enthusiastically, and keen to get ropes and pulleys attached to the giant tropical trees so they could get to the top of the canopy where no one had been before.

The last in the group were another pair of scuba divers, Billy and Gail Lemmon. Like their surname, they came across as slightly sour and Eva was sure she wouldn't have much to do with them. Billy was moaning now about the state of the minibus seats, the plastic leatherette covering being ripped and stained in many places. Gail's nasal voice joined in, griping about the stink of cigarette smoke as if the driver couldn't hear them or perhaps understand a little English. Eva was glad they'd be spending their time under the sea where she couldn't hear them.

The minibus engine growled and coughed before the motor caught and the minibus started up slowly, then moved with gathering rackety speed. Before long the suburban sprawl of Galanga was gone, along with the little children running alongside waving and cupping their hands for sweets, and the mangy dogs barking on the dusty roads. Inside they bumped up and down as the bus went over potholes. Eva bruised her forehead on the low ceiling and was forced to grab at Dan to keep her balance. He held her firmly until she sorted her seat. She smiled her thanks and tried to forget the warm feel of his muscled forearm. The heat was getting to her, that was all.

The bus climbed out of the valley and on to the north, where the jungle lay like green broccoli heads thickly bunched together with no space for ground to be seen. They stopped for a comfort break at a small village on the roadside. It was no more than a few wooden huts clustered together, surrounded by a fringe of banana trees and other exotic vegetation Eva couldn't identify. A crowd of small children and mangy curs came to greet them. Bob Grierson bought a strange green fruit and shared it out. Eva copied Daisy, who was scooping out what looked like frogspawn from the inside and eating it with gusto.

'Passion fruit,' she explained between mouthfuls.

'Really? It doesn't look like the ones I've seen in the supermarket,' Eva said doubtfully. However, she gamely took one that Dan offered her and tried it.

'It's fresh and a local variety,' Dan said, watching her with a smile. 'You won't have seen one like this before. Or tasted anything like it.' It was delicious and refreshing. He looked pleased at her obvious enjoyment of it.

Around them, the air was full of the noise of birds and buzzing insects. The forest was temptingly close. 'Do we have time to explore?' Eva asked.

Bob Grierson shook his head. 'No point stopping here. This is secondary rainforest and devoid of much interest. You can see that the banana plantations and the agriculture have quite spoiled it. Where we're headed is pristine rainforest, barely touched by man's interference.' He pointed to the soft, green-clad rolling ridges to the north.

Eva wiped her damp forehead. 'How much longer do we have to travel?'

'Another couple of hours,' Dan said, far too cheerfully in her opinion.

Then they were on the move again. Scattered villages passed them by, and on the far side of a winding mountain pass Eva saw houses on stilts, built precariously onto the cliff edge. Blue morpho butterflies butted against the minibus windows. The intense colour of their scales shimmered in the light. Christa and James were delighted, pointing out to the others how brown and drab the morphos were on their undersides, contrasting with the brilliance of the upper wings. Christa made notes in her book. Gail Lemmon rolled her eyes. Eva felt exhausted. The journey and the humid heat were too much. She longed to rest her head, but the only resting place was Dan's broad shoulder and she couldn't do that.

Eventually the minibus screeched to a halt in a belch of fumes. 'Are we there?' Eva asked with relief.

Dan leapt out of the bus and began to drag out rucksacks and equipment boxes from its underbelly. The other team members, equally experienced, were tightening buckles and securing items.

'Now we walk,' Dan told her, nodding beyond.

Eva looked where he indicated. The

minibus had come to rest in a small muddy circle at the edge of the rainforest. Beyond it was a wall of thick, moist and impenetrable jungle. She pulled on her rucksack and tucked her hair under the bandanna. She was determined not to ask Dan how long they were to walk. From the chatter in the bus on the way, she knew that the other team members had all worked together before and were very experienced in the rainforest habitat. Dan had worked with them all on other expeditions. Only Eva was new to the group. She'd quickly resolved in her own mind not to be a burden and not to stand out as a newcomer. She'd be helpful and resourceful and hope to fit in easily.

'Can you manage?' Dan asked.

Bob Grierson looked over at her. Eva was annoyed at Dan. She didn't want any doubts in the professor's mind about her. Besides, she didn't need any special concern from Dan. She wanted to be treated like any other member of Bob's team, not like some delicate

flower that had to have special attention.

'Of course I can,' she said, tilting her
chin up with more confidence than she
felt.

Now he looked amused. Why did he
seem to find her so entertaining? She
gritted her teeth and ignored him. The
others were moving single file into the
jungle. Brian Scopes was in the lead,
hacking through the vegetation with a
machete. Dan moved past her to help
him, a lethal-looking machete in his
hand. The thwack of blade on vines
rang out around them, mingling with
endless bird calls and the high,
repeating peep of some tiny rainforest
frog.

They moved in quietly, each person
concentrating on their footsteps and
breathing in the humid surroundings.
Eva was behind Gail Lemmon, the last
in the group. She couldn't help but be
aware of the forest to her back. In front
of her Gail was tutting as leaves slapped
at her face. Billy snapped back at her,

saying he couldn't help it. Eva tried to ignore their bickering, tried to envelop herself in the wild beauty of the place. A vine caught her foot and she stopped to unwind it and pull free. A primeval smell of ancient leaves and soil rose up from the forest floor. Looking up, she saw she was almost alone. Gail's back disappeared into the greenery ahead. For a moment it was just her and the jungle. She felt a surge of happiness closely followed by panic. Eva slid through the plants as fast as possible. She burst out into a clearing where the others stood.

'Here we are then,' Professor Grierson said. 'Let's get set up.'

Here? Eva didn't say it out loud. There was nothing to distinguish where they'd stopped from anywhere else. There was a wide brown river next to the clearing, moving sluggishly along. Half-submerged logs stuck out from the water like drowned limbs. A hunched-up bird squawked once and flew up from one on ragged, large wings.

'Right,' Bob Grierson went on, rubbing his hands together, 'tents over here, I think, and mess tent there. Better be smart about it before the local insects find us.'

The team set to work. Eva hung back, unsure what to do, before Daisy called her over and asked her to help her erect a tent.

'Thanks,' Eva said gratefully. 'Everyone seems to know what to do except me.'

'We're used to working together in a team,' Daisy told her cheerfully. 'It can be hard fitting into that. As long as you show that you are willing, you'll be alright. Dan will look after you.'

'There's no need for him to do that,' Eva retorted.

Daisy gave her a strange look. 'He's a good guy to have at your back in an emergency, you know. He'll never let you down.'

Eva laughed mirthlessly. 'Tell it to that poor girl Rose. He let her down, didn't he?'

Daisy started to say something, then bit her lip. Of course she couldn't defend him over his treatment of Rose, Eva thought triumphantly. They worked in silence then. The tents went up fast and the glade began to look less bleak.

'I'll get water, shall I?' Eva suggested. 'I'll make tea.' She wanted to get away from the awkwardness between her and Daisy. She went down to the water's edge with a pot from the supplies and dipped it in. Immediately there was a buzzing, and a cloud of brown insects hung in the air, not quite touching her but never leaving her. She swatted at them but they persisted with a high whining noise.

'Sweat bees,' Dan said, appearing beside her.

'Charming,' she replied, hitting at them ineffectually. 'How can I get rid of them?'

'You can't. You have to put up with them. And the mozzies.'

Eva slapped a mosquito off her arm, feeling its bite too late, a smear of blood left on her skin. 'So much for sleeping out under the stars.'

'Is that what you thought?' Dan grinned. 'Wait until you see the amount of mosquito netting Bob's brought for the tents.'

'Is it really necessary? Can't we just zip the tents?'

'You've a lot to learn, Eva. Getting mosquito bites isn't simply unpleasant. There's a risk of malaria. As camp doctor, my job is to minimise the risks to the team.' Dan stood up, picked up the full pot of water and strode off to the mess.

Eva made a face to his back. He'd been almost human for a minute there, but had reverted to being a know-it-all as usual. What did Rose see in him anyway?

Twilight descended surprisingly early. A stream of bats flew overhead and the eerie sounds of nightjars and owls began. Bob had lit a campfire and they sat round it cooking over its intense heat. The jungle had cooled and it was a strange sensation to feel the warmth of the fire on your face and arms while your back was cold and exposed to the night. Eva lapped it all up. This was her adventure and she wanted all of it.

Across from her on the other side of the licking flames, Dan's face was half illuminated, giving it a hawkish appearance. Her heart thumped. Did he have to be so gorgeous? Did he have to have this unwanted effect on her? She would keep away from him as far as possible in a small camp. Besides, she'd be away in the jungle looking for frogs and he'd be doing whatever doctors did when there were no patients to tend to. She wondered what he would be doing. Then told herself to stop. It was no concern of hers.

'That's it, folks. Early night,' Bob said. 'We'll get started with first light.'

Everyone rose from around the fire, murmuring goodnights. Eva rose too, suddenly tired and ready for her tent. Daisy had pointed it out to her earlier. She went inside, finding her way between the swathes of mosquito netting. Outside she heard Daisy laugh and Sam's deep voice, then the clang of metal and rustling of material as someone got into their tent. This was followed by a raised sharp complaint — Gail's voice from across the clearing — and Billy's angry reply. Thank goodness they were on the opposite side of the camp. Eva turned on her head torch and tried to find her pyjamas in her kitbag. She was ready for some time alone to think about the day. She slid down into the cotton sleeping bag on the camp bed. She shut her eyes.

There was a loud zipping noise close to her and her eyes opened wide. Curious, she knelt and peered out of the square of clear plastic on the tent side, which passed for a window. In the next tent she saw Dan. Most of him was a shadow through the material, illuminated by his torch. His outline was sharply defined.

He stripped off his shirt casually and Eva's breath caught in her throat. The outline of his torso was lean and muscled. She swallowed. Raw physical *want* of him submerged any other thought — to touch his skin, to run her hands down his flanks, to kiss his broad shoulder. She turned away to face the canvas side of her tent.

How would she stand it? To share a small jungle campsite with him for two months. Such close proximity, such intimate space. She didn't even *like* him! He was a cold-hearted monster, a bossy, arrogant . . . sexy, desirable and gorgeous man.

As if reading her thoughts, Dan spoke from the darkness beside her. She knew he was lying in his camp bed, not several feet away from her, separated only by the thin sides of their tents.

'Goodnight, Eva. Sleep well.'

She didn't trust herself to answer. She'd never manage to sleep now, so conscious as she was of his body so close to hers. His bed creaked as he turned over. It sounded so close she felt she could almost reach out and touch him. Or he could touch her. Eva shivered, but not with fear. She wasn't scared of him. She was annoyed at her body's traitorous impulses. Luckily, her mind was in control, Eva told herself with asperity. She sat up and shook out her hard, thin pillow vigorously. Beside her, or so it seemed, she heard his rhythmic breathing. The man was asleep already! No lingering desires tugging at him and keeping him awake then. He was indifferent to her. Piqued, she flung herself back onto the camp bed. She just knew she'd toss and turn all night.

With a sigh, Eva's eyelids dropped closed and sleep claimed her.

4

The camp routine settled down after a few days. They rose with the dawn, using the cackle and shriek of the birds as an alarm clock. Daisy and Sam had taken on the role of camp cooks and got the fire going and a blackened kettle of water boiling for bush tea and porridge. The rest of them sorted out kit for the day and discussed what they would be doing. Dan, as the team's doctor, was ready to help out where he could. So far his doctoring had only extended to attending mosquito bites on all of them, a sick stomach on the first day for Billy and a bruised leg for Sam where a branch had broken onto him.

Eva had made a couple of forays into the forest to find her poison arrow frog populations to study. She decided upon a riverside population to compare with the unusual cave-dwelling site. She was glad to be alone, working happily with notepad and pencil to describe the amphibian behaviour. Being with Dan in the intimacy of the camp was too much. At night she listened to his even breathing as she lay awake staring at the canvas roof and the web of netting, wishing she didn't find him so attractive physically. She didn't speak to him much unless it was necessary, but between them ran a current of live energy that spoke more than words. She wondered if he felt it too. Sometimes she felt his gaze upon her and she thought he felt hers, too.

This morning the divers were leaving for the coast. It was a few miles along a forest track and they had the anticipated pleasure of sleeping in huts for a few weeks with clean running water and insect-free interiors.

'Lucky them,' Daisy remarked to Eva, nodding towards Gail and Ann, who were laying out their scuba gear and checking it all. 'The huts are for rich tourists who want to 'rough it' for a while. Compared to this place, its five-star.' She chuckled as she said it.

Nothing got Daisy down. Eva smiled to herself. 'Can we visit?' she asked jokingly.

'Sure. We'll go and see them at the end of our work,' Daisy promised, lugging the kettle off the fire pole and pouring its contents into tin mugs. 'Can you throw a couple of water purifier tablets into this lot, please?'

Eva was doing just that when Dan appeared. 'Anyone fancy a look at the oil birds today?' He hunkered down to take a mug of tea and Eva felt the slight brush of his arm against hers. Her heart lurched and she moved away, annoyed with herself. He frowned at her questioningly.

'Oil birds?' she asked brightly. She didn't want to have to explain her behaviour.

'It's a rare chance to see them,' Daisy said. 'They echolocate like bats and live in dark caves. You should go with Dan.

I'd love to join you but I've promised Bob I'll help him mist-net humming-birds today. I think James and Christa have left already for the trees.'

'So what about it?' Dan asked when Eva didn't reply.

'Don't you have to do any doctor things?' she said curtly.

Dan shook his head. 'Not as yet. Everyone is shockingly healthy right now. So no excuses, we'll leave after breakfast.' He walked away, leaving Eva with her lips tightened. He was very sure of himself, ordering her about like that. Still, she did want to see the unusual birds and it was an opportunity to explore further into the jungle to places she mightn't see by herself.

She was packing a day sack when Bob Grierson caught up with her. He was dressed in light khaki jungle shirt and long trousers, with a butterfly net over one shoulder and a set of poles and netting which Eva guessed was the mist net for the hummingbirds.

'How are you, my dear? Finding the

tropics to your liking?'

'I love it,' she said honestly. 'I'm hoping to get some real results from my behavioural studies.'

'Enough for a scientific paper?' he asked, his blue eyes twinkling.

'Oh definitely,' she said, flustered. She wanted to be his best student ever, didn't she. If he wanted her to write a scientific paper then she had to get enough results to warrant writing one.

'Excellent. Gwendolin, your mother, really is the most wonderful woman. If you're half as good as her you'll be all right. Now, must hurry. We don't want to miss the heat of the day for the birds.'

There it was again: always the mention of the high-flying, utterly successful Professor Gwendolin Martinez. Eva was destined to stay in her mother's vast dark shadow forever. She couldn't compete. From what Bob Grierson had said, he only expected Eva to be half as good as her! She bit down on her lip and tried to ignore the sinking feeling in her stomach. Even her father believed it. Their last argument had ended with cruel words from him and Eva slamming out of the New York apartment swearing never to return.

'Whatever it is, it can't be that bad.'

She looked up to see Dan gazing at her strangely. She painted on a smile. 'I'm ready to go.' She slung her bag on her back and walked past him to the start of the forest trail. There was no way she was sharing her vulnerability with him. She could quite imagine him mocking her or worse, arrogantly telling her to grow up and get over it. No thanks. She'd handle her insecurities all by herself.

The divers had hacked an open track along the trail, which they followed for an hour before it forked into two. 'Left to the beach and right to the caves,' Dan said.

Eva wiped sweat from her forehead and swatted at the irritating bees which formed a little cloud around her. She nodded, having no breath to speak. The humid air was stifling.

'Another half hour at most. Can you make it?'

'If you can, then I can.'

'That's the spirit.' He grinned wickedly. 'I like an adventurous companion.'

'Is Rose adventurous?' Eva asked.

Dan's face darkened and he turned away, along the trail. 'She's had a few adventures.' He didn't elaborate and Eva didn't dare ask more. He looked thunderous and the machete was swinging viciously, mowing down the thick vines which stood in the way.

What was it with him and the delicate, beautiful Rose? Why had he dumped her when he was so obviously affected by her? Eva was certain he must love her. There was raw emotion when he spoke of her. Now that she'd decided that, the day had lost its colour. Which was stupid. It didn't matter what Dan did or who he loved. She didn't want him. And he most definitely didn't want Eva.

The caves were stunning. The black

entrance hole was in a wide glade with fallen mighty trees and rippling undergrowth. A river snaked across the ground in front of them and disappeared inside the cave. The sun beat down on them, glinting off the pale stone walls. She passed an elegant green lizard basking on a vine leaf and saw several morphos dancing in the sunbeams.

'Where are the oil birds?' she called over to where Dan was climbing a massive stone boulder to view the surroundings.

'Inside the cave, about a mile in,' he said, 'Do you want to eat before we go in?'

'No thanks, let's get going. And before you ask, yes I'm fine and I'm up for this.'

'I don't doubt it, but let me go first just in case.'

Eva made a face to his back. She could manage perfectly and it would've been fun to be first inside. 'How deep's the water?'

'Starts knee deep but soon gets to thigh level but no more,' he shouted over the gurgle and hiss of the river water. The noise was amplified by the echoing cave.

The first step into the water was cold. The river sucked at Eva's trousers with surprising power, guiding her along and into the bowels of the earth. She was hit by a stench as she turned on her head torch.

'Can you smell the birds?' Dan called.

She could barely see him up ahead. She tried to move faster but the water controlled her movements. Underfoot it was rocky and uneven, which slowed her down further. She concentrated on her feet, the light from her head torch weak and yellow as it reflected back from the silt grains in the water. She bumped into something large and solid. It was Dan.

'Hey, do you want to lead?' he asked, 'I'm being selfish; I've been here before. I remember the thrill of exploring these caves.'

'Great,' Eva exclaimed eagerly. Maybe he wasn't so bad after all.

She stepped carefully round him and went on. The stink of oil bird droppings got stronger. High up on each side of the cavern she noticed ledges stained with white streaks. They were nearly within reach of their quarry. She was going to suggest climbing up to the ledges when there was a movement in the murk ahead. Eva fumbled with her torch. A distance away there was a lower ledge in the cave wall diverting away into a side cave. The stone looked chossy in the torchlight, as if it would crumble to powder in places. An animal lay on the ledge. It was making a valiant attempt to stand but was too weak.

Eva waded towards it and away from the main cave.

'Eva! Don't go down there. It's all unexplored; it could be dangerous.'

'There's a . . . I think it's a wild pig . . . it's hurt. We need to get it out,' she shouted. The stream took her voice up and dissolved it.

She could hear Dan struggling to catch up with her and the splash and hollow ring of water and pebbles in his wake. Before he got to her, she was already reaching out of the water for a handhold on the slippery rock. The first jutting piece broke off in her fingers. She touched higher and found a crack to jam her fingertips into. With both hands she pulled up and swung her legs onto the narrow ledge. The pig gave a snort of panic. It was a soft brown colour with a cream collar and spots. It was a young forest peccary or quenk which had perhaps stumbled in to the cave and then been swallowed up by the force of the stream. It let her pick it up, its body limp and its heart racing. Its trotters trembled and kicked against her legs but there was no strength in them.

'What on earth are you doing?' Dan bellowed from the other side of the stream and below. He stood on a dry crescent of pebbles on the rim of the current, his head bent forward under the low cave roof. 'Put the damn thing down! The river's flooding. We need to get out.'

Sure enough, when Eva stared at the stream, the surface was rising, licking the cave walls wet higher and higher. For the first time, she heard the distant pounding of heavy rain on the faraway entrance. A tropical downpour in full torrent. The rainy season had started.

'It's hurt. We can't just leave it to drown.'

'*We'll* be drowning soon if we don't move the hell out of here. Now give me the quenk.'

She stared at him. He stared back.

He gave an exasperated sigh. 'I promise not to dump it in the water. Now give it to me.'

'Okay, but be gentle. It's terrified. You must take it out to the glade.'

'You should be terrified too,' he muttered, the water lapping hungrily at his legs.

'You shouldn't have wished for an adventurous companion then.' She grinned and stepped down gingerly. It should've been a safe move but her foot slipped and she gave a cry and went down until an agonising pain pierced her ankle.

'Eva!' Dan surged forward.

'My leg's stuck in the rocks!' she yelled.

Dan muttered something under his breath, gave her a grim look and told her he'd be back swiftly.

'I won't wander off,' she joked feebly. Her eyes watered with the pain in her leg. She wriggled but it only made it worse. Her ankle was well and truly jammed in an underwater crevice. The water level was rising fast. She forced herself to breathe evenly. Panic would help neither of them in here. She was suddenly glad it was Dan who was with her. Somehow she'd every confidence he'd get her out.

He was back quickly, the pig no longer in his arms, talking firmly but calmly. 'Listen to me, Eva. I'm going to try to free your foot. It might be sore but we've no time to waste. Are you with me?'

She bit down on her lip and nodded. His amber gaze was gentle but his brows were drawn together in concentration. He took a large gulp of air and went under the water. It was incredible how the stream had transformed into a raging deep river in minutes. All it had taken was a rainstorm. Tropical rainstorms were so heavy that centimetres of rain could fall in very little time. It was a hard introduction to Trinita's seasons. Eva twisted her mouth wryly. She cried out as Dan picked at the rock on her leg. He came up for air.

'I've nearly got you. Just one more rock to go.' Then he was submerged again. She screamed when the rock came loose. Dan grabbed her, wrapped her arm over his neck and half hoisted her towards the faint light of the cave entrance. She revelled in his closeness. It was safe and arousing and confusing and it was way better than focusing on her tender, bruised ankle. They swam and paddled against the current until, exhausted, they flung themselves from the cave and into the searing heat of the sun. The storm had passed as quickly as it had arrived. Everywhere around them, the jungle steamed as the rainwater vaporised.

Eva crawled away from the cave and sat dead centre of the glade. It was glorious to be in the open air. Dan came to sit beside her. For a moment they said nothing but listened to the roar of the river as it tumbled into the yawning cave mouth.

Then Dan turned to her, his voice angry. 'How could you be so irresponsible? You could've died in there.'

She was taken aback and her own anger surged. 'But I didn't. It was fine.'

'Of all the impetuous, stubborn . . . If I hadn't been there . . . '

'You sound just like my mother.' Eva's voice dripped with sarcasm. She hoped he wouldn't notice her legs trembling in delayed shock.

His face was so close to hers. She felt the warmth of his breath. For a second her lips parted in anticipation. Then he drew back from her and took in a deep breath. 'Come on. Let's get back to camp.'

Walking back, Eva couldn't stop thinking about that moment. What had happened in the glade? She was certain that Dan had been about to kiss her. She looked ahead as if his striding figure would give her a clue. He hadn't said anything to her since then other than warning her about a snake on the path and pointing out a hollow to avoid. Staring at his back, she knew that her attraction for him wasn't going away. If anything it was heightened further. She felt feverish with it.

Dan was glad when the camp came into view. It meant he could immerse himself in his duties and prepare his medical bag for the journey to the villages Bob had promised. It was a valid excuse to keep away from Eva. He had complicated things for himself by nearly kissing her. He had almost given in to an attraction that had simmered between them from the moment they'd met in the London coffee shop. He'd agreed to sponsor her trip to the island mostly to get back at Rose. It was sweet revenge. The look on Rose's face at the university party had been worth it. He wanted to hurt her just as much as she'd hurt him. He wasn't proud of it. But that moment in the glade — he was so close to touching those tempting lips with his and giving in to his impulse to kiss her. It had nothing to do with revenge on Rose — and everything to do with a rising desire for Eva.

Still, he had his body under control and he'd no intention of his heart being involved. He scanned the camp for her. She emerged from her tent, slender and sexy as hell. She pushed her outrageously thick, curly hair from her brow and tied it back. The movement stretched her shirt against her breasts, outlining their fullness, and Dan's body stirred.

Deliberately, he moved down to the river to gather wood. To distance himself from her for a while. He heard

Daisy's cheerful call and Bob's gruff voice as they returned to camp and Eva's answering laughter. He watched the water flow, bringing smoothed branches to him. Eva wasn't the cold-hearted calculating woman he'd painted her to be. Her actions in saving the quenk were pure madness, but showed a kindness he hadn't guessed at. She'd stood her ground at him, argued back. She could've died in the cave. They both could have. But she wasn't his responsibility any more than the other members of the team were. He had to remember that.

When he got back to England, he'd sort things out with Rose. He'd wanted to punish her and he had. But whatever he and Rose had together still needed to be resolved. Daisy was calling his name for mealtime. Dan picked up his sticks and went to join the others.

5

The waves at Maracca Bay were frothy and playful and the sun shone lemon-bright. Eva sat on a towel on the hot sand, her knees drawn up, resting her chin on them and watching the sea. Daisy and Sam frolicked in the surf and the sound of their laughter and screams as the waves crashed in made her sad in an indescribable way. There was a completeness about the couple that was enviable. They were both sociable, friendly people but they only needed each other. Eva was jealous. *Get over it*, she told herself. Somewhere in the world a soulmate was waiting for her. She'd find him sometime. *Twenty-six, getting on and no sign of him yet*. But if she did find him, would it end like her parents' marriage? She kicked up sand, annoyed. Here she was in this idyllic paradise and thinking gloomy thoughts. Enough. She was here to have fun. She scrambled up and ran down the beach to join them. *If only Dan was here.* Now where had *that* come from? He and Bob Grierson had gone to find the village elders deep in the forest. They'd been gone a week. In a weird way she missed him.

The sea was warm and salty and relaxing. Eva was content to splash about in the wavelets while Daisy screamed and Sam chased his wife in and out of deeper water. A local woman, balancing an improbably huge basket on her head, called out, offering them ripe mangoes. Eva bit into the orange flesh, tasting its sweetness. The woman smiled at her, the hem of her blue check dress dark with water as she walked the sea's edge selling her fruit.

'This is a bit naughty.' Daisy swam over to the shallows where Eva floated. 'But while the cat's away . . . '

'Bob won't mind, will he?' Eva asked nervously. She was intent on making a good, long-lasting impression on him, with the hope he'd tell her mother what a good student she was.

'Who cares!' Daisy laughed, tilting her face to the sun happily.

'Cat's out of the bag anyway, to continue your analogy,' Sam interrupted, nodding up the beach to where the palm trees fringed the dust road.

Eva followed his gaze. Her heart began a little dance. Emerging from the trees were two men. Dan and Bob waved to them. Eva saw Dan was unshaven with tired eyes. She smiled at him. There was a flicker of surprise in his response but he smiled back then. They met at the makeshift picnic spot where they'd dumped their towels and bags.

'We guessed where you'd be when we found the abandoned camp,' Bob boomed, shaking a finger warningly at Daisy. 'You'll be making up for this, Mrs Kew. Extra hummingbird catches.' But he wasn't serious.

Dan sat down beside Eva. 'You don't mind sharing, do you?' His voice was gravelly with fatigue.

'What happened? Haven't you slept?' she asked, making a place for him.

Bob Grierson rubbed his face. She realised he was exhausted too.

'We had a spot of bother with the locals. I was taking Dan to meet with two village elders that I've known for some years. The villages aren't far apart but they're both quite deep into the jungle. They don't have a lot to do with the outside world and certainly not with foreigners. There is an unusually high percentage of Harrap virus in the communities, which is why I chose these villages, but what I didn't expect was to be met with open hostility. They basically ran us out of town with machetes and spears raised threateningly. We didn't stop to camp last night. We kept moving all night in case they caught up with us.'

'Why were they hostile?' Daisy asked. She opened bottles of fresh fruit juice and handed them to the two men, who drank them gratefully.

Bob shrugged his shoulders help-lessly. 'No idea. My grasp of the indigenous language is tenuous to say the least. I usually get by on gestures. But I didn't need a translator for the chief's gestures yesterday!'

'It's a pity Rose isn't here. She knows the lingo,' Daisy said, then stopped rather suddenly. She looked at Dan. 'Sorry.'

He was so tired, he didn't react. 'Rose is an expert in the indigenous languages of South America,' he explained to Eva.

She would be. Eva was surrounded by experts. It came as no surprise that Rose was one too. Eva felt her familiar inadequacy cloak her. Her mother would be impressed by Rose. Dan must like super-intelligent women. That ruled her out. She struggled all the time to be a good-enough scientist. Not that she wanted to be 'ruled in' by Dan, whatever that meant. She wanted . . .

'Eva?'

'What!' It came out sharper than she intended. When she looked up from her negative mulling she found there was just her and Dan. Daisy, Sam and Bob were down at the sea, paddling along to the jutting peninsula at the end of Maracca Bay, their figures gradually getting smaller.

'You were miles away,' he remarked softly.

'Sorry. Was it scary, your encounter with the villagers?' A change of subject. Clever idea, Eva Martinez. Brush your worries aside as usual. Her mind wandered to the letter in her day sack. Later. She'd read it again later. Perhaps she'd misinterpreted it.

'Having a sharp machete brandished in your face was daunting,' he said; then, grinning, he added, 'I didn't know Bob was so athletic.'

'You had to run from them?'

'Not quite, but we were walking pretty fast when we left the village. I've no idea what spooked them so much. Daisy's right. If only we'd had an interpreter.'

There was a silence between them

then. Eva thought of Rose. She knew Dan was too. Did he love her? Was he regretting his rash decision not to marry her? Not that it meant anything to Eva. It was none of her concern.

'I'm sorry,' she said.

'For what?'

'I know how much it meant to you to get into the villages and give out medicines to the people. And to try to find your cure to Harrap.'

'I was itching to get in there and fix people,' he said. 'While Bob was arguing with the chief, I could see lots of skin and eye conditions easily sorted. There was one kid who had what looked like a badly mended broken arm. It was frustrating.'

'You really care about them,' Eva said. It struck her when he was speaking about his medicine there was no trace of the bossiness, the over-confidence she'd so hated about him. Had he changed then? Or had she imagined it in the first place?

'Yes, I care. That's why I wanted to

be a doctor. To help people. Why else?' He sounded amused at her.

Funnily, it didn't make her angry any more. He wasn't laughing at her. She even sort of liked the fact she could make him smile.

'Did your family want you to be a doctor?' she asked curiously. He hadn't mentioned parents or siblings, and no family had turned up at the party.

'It runs in the family,' Dan told her. 'My mother was a GP and my older brother and his wife are both consultants at city hospitals. It was assumed I'd do the same. Luckily I found myself interested in medicine early on, so I was happy to follow in Tom's wake.'

'Are your parents proud of you?' The question stuck in her throat painfully.

'Yes, I suppose so. Never asked myself that. It's more important that I'm happy, isn't it? Making your parents proud ... well, it's an odd way to expend energy. They're happy doing what they're doing. Tom's content as a pig in mud and I'm okay too.'

Eva considered this. She'd been striving to make her parents happy all her life. To be told by Dan that she'd wasted her energy on it was an interesting concept. It had become a habit over the years. She judged her happiness and success by what they thought of her.

'What about you?' he was asking. 'Have you parents, brothers and sisters?'

'I'm an only child, which is probably lucky.' Eva let a grasp full of sand trickle like brown sugar through her fingers.

'Lucky?' Dan lay back, his arms behind his head, listening to her, one eyebrow cocked at her strange comment.

'Yes, I would've hated for other kids to live the way I did when I was growing up. There was so much arguing and slammed doors and frosty silences in our house. It came as a relief when my parents split up.'

'What age were you?' Dan asked gently.

'I was nine. I think I understood even then that my father had had an affair with a much younger woman and I guess my mother threw him out. They would've split anyway; they could never agree on anything. So I spent my childhood travelling between London and New York, never quite sure where I belonged.'

'Poor little Eva.' Dan sounded genuinely sad for her.

'Don't worry, poor little Eva grew up,' she said with a bitter smile. 'You'll have heard of my mother, Professor Gwendolin Martinez?'

Dan shook his head. 'Don't think so. Should I have?'

Eva was absurdly pleased to find someone so unimpressed by her mother's name. Of course Dan didn't work in the field of zoology, so why should he have heard of her? Still, it was refreshing. She reached over to get a drink from her bag. She touched paper. The letter. Her stomach lurched. She had an impulse to screw it up and cast it into the sea. It wouldn't change the contents though.

She looked round to Dan to ask him more about the jungle villages. He was fast asleep. She studied him. He was gorgeous, there was no denying it. She leaned towards him. His lashes were long and black against his tanned skin. They'd be the envy of any girl. She giggled at that, then stifled it in case he woke. With his intense tawny gaze shuttered, he was oddly vulnerable. His lips were curved as if he was amused in his sleep. She was so close, if she wanted she could touch her mouth to his. A rope of longing coiled in her. Then a tiny cough made her start.

Daisy stood there. Beyond her, Eva saw Sam and Bob making their way back to them.

'We're going to take the local bus back,' Daisy said, politely not mentioning what she'd seen.

Eva blushed. She had practically devoured Dan with her study of him. It was embarrassing that Daisy had got back right then.

'Why don't you wait with Dan and drive the jeep back? It's a pity to wake him,' Daisy suggested kindly.

They had come to the beach by bus, since Bob and Dan had driven the jeep as far as they could before trekking in to the villages. Obviously they'd then driven back to Maracca once they found the camp empty. Eva wondered where James and Christa had got to. They'd declined the outing to the beach in favour of climbing into the canopy once more.

'Okay. See you, then.' Eva waved the three of them off at the road where an ancient bus had appeared, already crushed with passengers.

She walked slowly back to the beach, enjoying the solitude. The mango-seller had gone and the few other people swimming had vanished too. There was just her and a sleeping Dan and the wide ocean. The sun was dipping in a cream sky and twilight was seeping in. She heard the change in bird calls as the day birds quietened and their night cousins woke up and announced their presence. A bell bird rang its song deep within the tree-clad slopes backdropping the beach. Eva found branches and sea drift twigs and set a fire. One of her new skills, taught by Daisy. The crackling orange glow was comforting. Above her, one by one the glittering stars appeared, until the heavens were laden with jewels in navy velvet. She was utterly, completely happy at that instant. This was how she'd imagined the tropics to be. Only better, she added. Her image hadn't included an attractive male at her side.

As if he'd heard her, Dan woke with a start and sat up. 'What did I miss? Where is everyone?'

Eva fed the fire a few more twigs. 'You fell asleep. It seemed mean to wake you so the others have gone back. We can follow when we're ready.'

He stood and stretched. She tried not to notice where his shirt had raised up, exposing a six-pack stomach, lean and hard.

'Can you fish?' he asked.

'Eh, no. Not much call for it in London. Or New York, come to think of it.'

'You've missed out. Come on.' He grabbed her arm and pulled her up.

'Don't you need a fishing rod? And bait?' Eva asked vaguely, trying to remember stuff she'd seen on television. Actually her father had taken her fishing once at the coast in New Jersey. It had ended in tears. Hers and Nancy's.

'What?' Dan was waiting impatiently, hands on hips.

How did the man get so much energy all of a sudden? Amazing what a cat nap could achieve.

'I was remembering a fishing trip I made with my Dad when I was about twelve.'

'Ah, so you have fished before. Great. You can hook the bait then.' Dan flourished fishing twine and metal tobies from his bag. As she watched, he tied twine to long sticks and used a complicated knot to attach the hooked baits.

'A Boy Scout. How wonderful,' she said under her breath. At least he was joking about the bait.

'You won't be so dismissive when you're eating freshly cooked fish for your dinner,' Dan said with a grin. His teeth were astonishingly white against his dark skin and the darker night. 'Anyway, you were telling me about your dad.'

Was she? Dan was a good listener, she decided. She'd told him more about her parents than she usually let slip to friends. She followed him down the beach, her soles feeling the cooling sands. A warm, tropical breeze ruffled the sea surface. He thrust an improvised fishing pole into her hand and cast his own line. It landed and sank with a satisfying plop.

'Yes, well, my father decided to do a little bonding with me that summer,' Eva said, watching her own line tug with the swell. 'He'd read too many American novels maybe. Anyway, he came up with the idea that we'd go fishing. At twelve I wasn't too happy with that. I was into makeup and fashion and shopping. We lived in New York, for goodness sake. And my father wanted us to leave the city and go fish for smelly, slimy creatures on a muddy bank in the middle of nowhere. I kicked up a stink but he was adamant. Not only that, but he'd invited Nancy. This was the girl he'd left my mother for. And yes, she was every cliché you can imagine. She was half his age, blonde cheerleader material and not the smartest. I didn't get it. My father is a professor of immunology. Nancy, as far as I could make out, hadn't even finished college.'

'Sounds like a recipe for disaster,' Dan said, his pole bending to a bow curve.

'The day ended with me pushing Nancy into the drink. Needless to say, we never went fishing again.' Eva's own pole bent and she felt a tug.

'How long did Nancy stay in your life?' Dan asked. He was walking backwards onto the shore, guiding the wriggling line.

'She's still there. She and my father got married years ago and actually, she's an okay step-mother.' Eva screamed in delight as her pole shuddered and a fish jumped out of the surf attached to her line.

'Bring it in! Bring it in!' Dan barked, 'Not like that. Run back, guide the line. The line, Eva!'

'Stop bossing me!' she snapped. The line zigzagged alarmingly and the fish almost fell off.

Dan tried to grab her pole. She twisted away from him. 'Get off!' she yelled. 'It's mine. I'm bringing it in.'

It was over in minutes. The fish flopped onto the shore. Eva punched the air with triumph.

'Well done,' he said. 'Am I allowed to take your fish now?'

'If it means your gutting them, then

yes please. I only want to see it again once it's a harmless grilled fillet on my dinner plate.'

Dan bowed mockingly. 'Your wish is my command, your Ladyship.' He took both catches and whistled as he went to the fire.

The fire cast flickering shadows, which licked over the empty plates and Eva's toes as she stretched out as contentedly as a cat. Somehow her head had landed up resting on Dan's midriff. It felt right, especially as he absent-mindedly was playing with her curls. It struck her that she'd told him an awful lot about herself, too much really. While he had told her very little. She didn't dare mention Rose for fear of him freezing her out. But she wanted to. What had gone so terribly wrong between them that he had left her? It was none of her business.

His fingers moved from her hair to the nape of her neck, massaging gently. It made her skin shiver nicely. She rolled, seeking a new position, and he bent his head and kissed her. He tasted of sea and salt. Little tendrils of desire licked her, then ignited as his kisses deepened. He lifted his head to look into her eyes.

'This wasn't meant to happen.'

'Do you regret it? It's only kisses after all,' she said, trying for a light tone and succeeding.

'I don't want to complicate things,' Dan replied. 'Do you? We're getting to be friends, I hope, but it would be a shame to destroy that.'

Eva didn't answer. She threw another twig on the fire instead. Did she want to just be friends? Maybe that was all that was possible. After all, Dan had only emerged from a serious relationship with Rose recently. If he wanted to mend it, she didn't want to be the one standing in his way.

Her skin was cooling in the night air. The fire had fallen to grey ash and it was time to go.

It was safe in the jeep, like a cocoon, as Dan drove them back. The jungle plants brushed the vehicle's windows and once a forest deer ran across the road in front of them. Dan took her hand and held it until a rut in the tarmac forced him to change gears. Eva's thoughts from earlier returned. Her envy of Daisy and Sam, her want of a soul mate. Could Dan be 'the one'?

His voice was like a slap of icy water. 'Bob was asking me about you. If you're up to the job. Any idea why?'

The damn letter! Her domineering mother. Gwendolin had written to Bob Grierson about Eva. She was sure of it. She could almost hear her mother's voice, justifying it. *I was concerned about you darling. Don't take on a project if you might fail at it. I'm letting Bob know about Connecticut.*

Eva was wide awake. The jeep was no longer a cocoon. And she most certainly didn't need a soulmate. She needed to remember why she was here. To prove to her mother, and her father, that she was good enough. As good as them, if not better. She had to get Bob

Grierson's approval for her project.

'No idea why he'd ask that,' she lied. There was a pause during which only the grind of the old jeep engine could be heard. 'By the way, this . . . attraction between us — it's not serious, right? I mean, once we leave Trinita, we go our separate ways. And you're right, it would be a shame to mess up our friendship.'

He didn't answer for a moment. Then, 'Of course. If that's what you want.' He looked straight ahead at the road and she couldn't read his emotion. But it made sense that he agreed with her. After all, she was convinced he'd get back with Rose eventually. Once they'd sorted their disagreement.

'Just so we both know where we stand,' Eva trailed off weakly. She stared out the window into the black, seeing her own pale reflection, all large eyes and sad mouth.

'You've made it very clear,' Dan said evenly. His knuckles whitened on the steering wheel but Eva wasn't watching.

In the tent she lit the tilley lamp to read her letter. She hadn't misinterpreted it. Her mother was coming out to Trinita. She worried about Eva alone with that man. Meaning Dan, presumably. She wasn't convinced that Eva could manage the frog project. But Gwendolin could help her. Together they'd get the results. At the end of the letter, a scribbled PS. *Your father sends his love apparently. Nancy called.*

Even now, her parents couldn't bear to talk to each other directly. Nancy was the go-between. Strangely, Gwendolin had come to terms with her replacement and used Nancy as the communicator when required. Usually about Eva.

I've written to Bob to let him know to expect me arriving. I know he's concerned about you. Remember he's a perfectionist. You have to get the goods one hundred percent. I can help you.

Concerned perfectionist? A description of her mother if ever there was one. But Gwendolin was on her way to

Trinita and there was nothing Eva could do. She sighed and flung the crumpled ball of paper up in the air. It bounced off the canvas ceiling and fell under her bed.

6

The divers had it good. They were sharing a beach hut, which was one of a cluster owned by an eco-holiday company to house rich tourists who wanted an experience off the beaten track. Dan had been called over because Gail was sick. He sat under an artfully arranged palm leave shelter, listening to the beat of the ocean waves and the nasal whine of Gail's complaints. Beyond her he saw Brian and Ann in their wetsuits heading for the reefs. Billy hovered anxiously in the shelter, glancing at his wristwatch when he thought Gail couldn't see him. Gail was repeating her description of her skin rash and blaming the rough accommodation for it.

Dan let her moan. Her rash wasn't serious and he had a tube of antihistamine cream ready to give her. But his thoughts were away in the jungle where

Eva was. She'd gone early this morning to her study site after a scant breakfast. She looked tense and worried and he'd wondered whether she regretted their kisses last night. But she'd greeted him with a smile and he thought then it wasn't him that was making her unhappy. He'd held back from asking. If she wanted to share, then she would. Asking her if she was okay would only annoy her. He'd made that mistake before. She was as independent and prickly over it as possible. For some reason she had to do everything by herself. What was she trying to prove? He was briefly irritated by that, but not for long when he saw how pale she was under her recently acquired tan.

'Are you okay?' he asked anyway.

She frowned at him and looked over at where Bob was scooping up a bowl of porridge before answering tightly, 'Why shouldn't I be? Now excuse me, I must get to my study site.'

He watched as she shouldered her rucksack and slung her binoculars round her neck. Then she walked away down the track. He felt an odd sense of loss when she rounded the curve and was gone behind the dense foliage. Having decided they should just be friends, he was shocked to discover how much he liked her. He should've been relieved when last night in the jeep she'd echoed him, telling him it wasn't a serious attraction between them and it would end when they left the island. So why had it felt wrong? As if she'd punched him in the gut.

'Dan? Are you even listening?' Gail's edgy whine brought him back to reality.

He gave her the cream with instructions on when to apply it and then was waylaid by Billy showing him a scraped shin where coral had scored it. Coral cuts don't heal easily, so it was good Billy had told him. Gail didn't wait for her husband. She went to get her gear. Then the handset in Dan's pack bleeped. He could hardly make out Daisy's crackled message. Christa had fallen while climbing. Dan was needed back at camp immediately.

*   *   *

It was peaceful at the bottom of the cave. Above her, there was a wide circle of light and a welcome view of the sky. The small colony of poison arrow frogs lived on the cave floor within the circle of light. Further afield, where the darkness lingered and the cave narrowed into tunnels, there were bats and amphisbaenids and giant cockroaches and rats. But in the centre there were only frogs. To get to them, Eva had to climb down the rocky cave wall, holding on to vines and knotted roots. There was a natural staircase of wide ledges to place feet and it wasn't too heart-stopping to get up or down.

She got out her video camera and recorded two males wrestling in territorial combat. She tried to immerse herself in the behavioural studies but her mind kept drifting to Connecticut and Gwendolin's threat to let Bob know about it. She didn't want the others in the team to find out. Especially Dan. Why it mattered what Dan thought about her, she didn't analyse. The trouble was that she *liked* him. When had that happened? She supposed she could like him just as long as it didn't deepen into anything else. *And it won't*, she promised herself. It was too important to work at her research and focus on that.

How would Bob Grierson react when he found out about the Connecticut debacle? Automatically she counted the aggression postures of the two males, the number of actual contacts made and how many times each was flipped to the ground. She could already guess the winner. But she was thinking of that summer in New England and the high hopes she'd had for it. She was a second-year student looking for a summer job. She was going to work in a shop and then travel around Europe like everyone else that summer. There was a boyfriend, long hair and straggly hippy beard, Zack..Zane . . . Zig, that was it. Offbeat name and offbeat guy. But she was into him big time. How young and naïve she'd been.

She remembered her father calling her in. 'I've got you a job. Friend of mine needs a student to observe copperheads up in the backwoods in Connecticut. You start Monday.' His grey eyes and curly dark hair were so like her own. His spontaneity too. How like her father to conjure this up at the wink of an eye and not even to warn her.

'What if I don't want it?' she asked petulantly, thinking already that Zig wouldn't like it. He wanted her to trail with him to southern Europe and into Morocco. She guessed why. He loved his smokes.

'Don't be ridiculous. Of course you're going. I've arranged a lift for you. Don't let me down, Eva,' he warned. 'I've promised Gil you'll do a fine job.'

So reluctantly, off she went to study one of Connecticut's two venomous snakes. Zig arrived a few days later, having hitched up. But he soon got bored of the endless birch trees and the few snakes they encountered. He left her for Morocco and for some girl with long blonde hair and tie-dyed skirts who arrived in a beat-up combi van and whisked him away. Eva cried for days. Then she left, too. She didn't tell her father, but was unprepared for his rage when she came home.

'You've let me down. You've let yourself down. What were you thinking? I've had Gil phoning me asking what's going on. He went up there to check on you and you'd vanished. Did you want to make a fool of me?' he shouted. He'd added another few choice words in Spanish, a language he'd learned at his mother's knee and passed his love of on to Eva. Now he used it to wound.

She packed and fled back to London, where Gwendolin had given her a frosty welcome. 'Thing is, darling, I was planning quite a bit of work time. You know I like the house silent for that. Why are you back from the States so soon?'

It was one thing her parents managed to agree on. Eva had let them both down badly. She was unlikely to get another study post as she was unreliable. Didn't she know her reputation would be damaged by what she'd done? And their reputations too. Her father had never quite forgiven her. In their recent argument, he'd brought it up again to wave in her face. He wanted Eva to settle in America near him and Nancy and had sourced two potential jobs for her. When Eva protested that she hadn't decided where to live or when to settle down, he got upset. She was selfish; she had to think of her family. He and Nancy weren't getting any younger. It'd be good to have her nearby.

It ended in an argument with him flinging at her that she'd always favoured Gwendolin, and her shouting back that he should've thought about the effects before he had an affair and destroyed her mother and his marriage. That pulled him up short before he told her she was never going to amount to much if she didn't watch out.

Connecticut was an example of how badly she was able to mess up. They hadn't spoken since.

★   ★   ★

The first person Dan met on his return to the camp was Christa. She was rigging up ropes on a massive buttress trunk and waved cheerfully to him. 'Christa? I had a call saying you were hurt. Daisy called.'

'Daisy called about me? I don't think so. Yeah, I did fall a wee bit but not too far. Just got a shock, no bruises. I don't think Daisy was calling about that, was she?'

Dan shrugged. Christa shinnied up the smooth bark like a monkey. High above her, the leaves were shaking and

James shouted down to her to hurry up. Dan left them to it, puzzled by Daisy's garbled message. What was so important she called him back?

When he got into the camp there was a large group of people standing there. He didn't recognise any of them. Daisy was gesturing frantically to him from the opposite side of the glade. As he walked towards her, the group opened out. There was a woman in the centre and she turned to him and smiled. It was Rose.

7

'Why are you here, Rose?'

The group had dispersed to set up camp nearby and only Rose remained. She tilted her face to him. She was beautiful in a classically English way: flawless porcelain skin which so far had avoided any impact of the strong Trinita sun. Big, clear blue eyes and long, straight blonde hair that reached the middle of her back. Dan's main emotion on seeing her was regret. This was the woman he'd wished to marry. He'd fallen in love with her the moment he met her. And she'd thrown that love away carelessly.

'The official reason?' she smiled, showing perfect white teeth that only money could buy. 'Daddy's funding my private expedition to record the local languages on Trinita and the other islands in the archipelago.'

'What convenient timing,' Dan said, not bothering to hide the sarcasm. 'Bob must be delighted you're here.'

She laughed prettily. 'Bob needs an interpreter — one who can speak to the locals, not just spout some Spanish. He wasn't averse to some extra project funding either.'

'And the unofficial reason you're here?' Although he knew the answer.

'To win you back. If you'll just let me, I know I can convince you to give me a second chance. Everyone deserves that, don't they? I made a mistake . . . '

'And how is Sean these days?' Sean, who had been Dan's best friend through medical school. Sean, whom Dan had found with Rose one afternoon in his bedroom.

'He went back to Ireland. I'm . . . we're . . . not in touch any more. Dan?' Unshed tears shimmered in her blue eyes.

'I wish you hadn't come here. I'm busy as the expedition doctor. That's what I'm concentrating on.' Dan turned away from her.

She called to his back, 'How's your *girlfriend*? She's hardly your type. Don't lie to me and tell me you love her, Dan Adams, because I know you don't. You still love me!' Her voice rose shrilly.

Dan paused until she'd finished. Then he walked steadily away. The truth was, she could still affect him. And he didn't want her to see that. His hurt was so raw, a wound that might be healing but could be ripped open so very easily. Did she deserve a second chance? Did he still love her?

Eva was satisfied with her day's results. Her territorial males had danced and wrestled well and she'd found some tadpoles of the same species which she'd gathered in a jar for observation. The sky above the cave was dimming and the first wave of bats had flown out, ready for a night's hunting. Soon there would be a constant black stream of them. She knew there were literally thousands roosting in the cave system. She felt invigorated. The day's work had dissipated any worries about her abilities. She was confident that she had enough results to produce a really good scientific paper on poison arrow frog behaviour. Not only that, but she'd discovered some new behaviours in the male fighting stances that she was pretty sure hadn't been detailed before.

With excitement, she gathered her equipment together. She would mention it to Bob tonight. Even if Gwendolin had written to him about Connecticut, she could surely demonstrate that she'd grown up since then. Her results from this trip would speak for themselves. Even her mother must be proud of her then. Which made her think of Dan and what he'd said about his own family. He didn't work to make them proud. He worked to make himself happy. If only she could emulate that. If only she could stop worrying about what they thought of her. How lovely it would be to have someone who believed in her whatever she did. And why did that take her right back round to thoughts of Dan again?

'I am being ridiculous,' she told herself. 'He's not for me. In another month he'll be gone.' A pair of round, golden eyes blinked at her in the dark in agreement. Some kind of owl which took off on heavy wings at her approach.

Eva pulled up on the vines until she crawled over the lip of the top of the cave. The jungle night was in full swing, with whoops of monkeys high up above her and catcalls and incessant peeping from amphibians looking for mates. She was looking forward to the campfire and the camaraderie of the team sitting round it, swopping stories of their day. James had turned out to be an entertaining raconteur and had them in stitches over descriptions of what he and Christa had found in the canopy. She liked to sit beside Dan, enjoying his proximity and feeling safe and content with the others.

Even Bob Grierson didn't seem so frightening now that she'd seen him in his pyjamas with morning hair stuck up all over the place, grumbling for his porridge.

She turned on her head torch and its thin beam struck the jungle leaves into gold. Then she was up and over the edge and onto flat ground. She started walking the way back to the camp, then stopped. Was it this way? She was disorientated in the velvety darkness. The weak beam of the torch made the rest of the night even darker. It cloaked her like a damp cloth. She was mistaken — she needed to head in the opposite direction, surely. Eva took a moment to take her battered paper map from her trouser pocket. She carried it always in fear of an occasion just like this one. She scrutinised it, tracing her path from the camp to the research location with her fingertip. Yes, that was it — she had to go a little way north before she turned off onto the joining trail back to camp. She was sure of it.

It was hard not to listen to the sound of her own breathing as she walked quickly. She tripped once and forced herself to slow down. No point turning up with a broken ankle. Dan wouldn't be pleased, to say the least. Ahead of her there was a band of silence, like a break in the ocean of plants. Her sixth sense came into its own. She hesitated. To her left there was a rustling in the trees. Fear of a jaguar made her hurry on. Only her foot stepped out into thin air.

With a frightened cry she flung herself backwards, hitting the ground hard and making her teeth rattle. She sat up and crawled gingerly forward. A great gash appeared in front of her. She stuck out her hand, feeling for the soil. But there was none. She was right on the edge of a huge emptiness. She looked at her map, angling the head torch to read it and flicking away the flies that hovered on the light's edge. There it was, sketched on the hand-drawn map. Bob's very own details of local features. Lunara Gorge. It spread across the pulpy paper like a black insect. Bob had put in an exclamation mark beside it as a warning.

Eva saw she was walking in totally the wrong direction. Lunara Gorge was not anywhere near the camp. She had to turn on her own trail and head back. She waited for the growl of a jaguar but there was nothing. It was her imagination in overdrive. She tucked the paper back in her pocket, hoping she wouldn't need to use it again, and started retracing her steps.

There was a fire when she got back and Daisy was cooking over the big, blackened pot, but there was an extra person sitting with the others. Eva did a double take. It was Dan's Rose. She watched from the edge of the jungle as Rose gave a peal of tinkling laughter. James jumped up animatedly. He was in the middle of one of his stories. She searched for Dan. He was there, sitting quietly next to Sam, staring into the flames. Christa was telling her husband to calm down and helping Daisy serve up. It was a cosy scene. Complete. For a moment, childishly, she thought, *They don't need me now. They've got Rose.* She forced herself to go in to join them.

'Oh here she is.' Rose stood up to greet her. 'Dan's student. How lovely. I must congratulate you on getting my job as trip translator. You must be so glad.' She made a pretence of shaking Eva's hand, letting her sharp nails dig ever so slightly in. She leaned in to air kiss Eva's cheeks and whispered, 'He isn't yours. He's mine.'

Eva was aware of Daisy and Christa looking approvingly at Rose as if to say, how gracious Rose is. She took her hand back as quickly as she could, the skin on her palm smarting from the other woman's nails. Rose reminded her of her study frogs — so stunningly beautiful, yet deadly. Eva wanted to tell her she was wrong — that there was nothing going on between her and Dan the way Rose was implying. But then she didn't owe Rose anything, not while she was acting so nastily. Eva went automatically to sit with Dan in her usual spot. But Rose was too quick. She slid gracefully into Eva's place. Eva hesitated.

'Sit with me,' Rose said, patting the space between her and James, who looked disappointed. 'I want to know all about you. How you and Dan met, how he became your sponsor. It's so ideal, so . . . fast.'

Eva had no choice. Daisy gave her a bowl of soup and a sympathetic wink, and she sat.

'So go on then,' Rose prompted. 'How did you two meet? It must've been rather sudden. After all, Dan had jilted me only weeks before you met.'

'Rose,' Dan warned.

'No really. It's fine. I simply want to know.' She gave another tinkling laugh that was meant to sound carefree. She was beginning to grate on Eva's nerves. Luckily at that moment, Bob Grierson joined them and started talking loudly about going back to the villages. He was planning a trip the next day and taking Rose as the interpreter. Who else wanted to come?

'Are you sure that's wise?' Daisy asked, grabbing at Sam, who had immediately volunteered to accompany Bob. 'Isn't it dangerous going back to the villages? They were hostile. Dan?' she said, looking for support.

Dan shook his head. 'She's right, Bob. The chief was none too pleased to see us. Next time it could be worse than a few waving machetes. And I don't think Rose should go.'

'I'd like to see the villages,' Eva interrupted. 'Maybe you caught them on a bad day. After all, Bob's been visiting the villages for years without problems.'

Dan glared at her. She noticed he didn't then go on to say she shouldn't go. Only precious Rose was too delicate to take.

'Eva's quite right,' Bob said, lighting one of his evil-smelling cigars and leaning back relaxed at the fireside. 'I know these guys. Whatever was spooking them last week is probably long gone. I say we go. Volunteers only. If you want to stay here, that's fine too.'

There was a brief silence before everyone spoke at once. Eva was pleased at Bob's praise. And glad to have annoyed Dan, who was still giving her a black look. He wasn't going to dictate what she did or where she went. If Rose liked being bossed about by Dan, that was her look out.

'We'll be wild camping overnight to get there and back,' Dan said. 'It won't be pleasant with all the insect life and no mosquito netting. And if there is trouble in the village, we may need to leave with haste. Is everyone prepared for that? Rose? Have you actually travelled in the tropics before?'

'You know I have, darling. I've been on loads of trips to the Caribbean and the Bahamas. Then there was that lovely holiday in Hawaii that Daddy gave me for my birthday one year.

That's tropical, isn't it?'

'And you must have travelled to study the South American languages,' James said admiringly. Eva caught Christa's pained expression.

'Well, no, not exactly,' Rose said, inspecting her crimson fingernails. 'It's desk study mainly. I use tapes that explorers and other linguists have brought back. Johnny Glaser, you know; he's the best etymologist around. Records all sorts of things.' She smiled at James, who smiled back automatically. Who could resist such pale beauty? Eva felt too tall and too swarthy in comparison. If Rose was Dan's sort of woman, then Eva most certainly wasn't.

'That's settled then.' Bob slapped his knee. 'We'll keep it a small band. Dan, we'll need you in case of any medical emergencies, and you'll get to hold a clinic in the village of course. Rose, you come as translator for the local dialects. Eva, you can be our Spanish translator if we need one, and you can also help me get samples of insect species around the village. Anyone else?'

James said he would go too. There were butterflies which were only found near settlements and it would be a rare chance to study and collect them. Christa pursed her lips and said nothing but looked deeply unhappy. Eva wondered about the couple. They'd appeared to be perfect together but Rose, so recently arrived, had opened a division between them. And was relishing it. She made a point of teasing James about his climbing and even pretended to feel the strength of his muscled arm. Was she trying to make Dan jealous? If so, it wasn't working. Dan was ignoring her, talking to Bob about the trip.

Christa got up and went to her tent. Daisy gave Eva a worried glance, then followed Christa. Sam whistled and busied about, tidying up the pots and dishes.

'I'll help you,' Eva offered, glad to get away from the atmosphere.

'Great, you carry those and I'll take the pan. Down to the river.' Sam nodded.

'Let me. I need the experience.' Rose joined them and took a single plate. Behind her, James's mouth drooped in disappointment.

The river was black and sinister, like a sinuous snake. Eva scrubbed the plates with grit. Rose dropped hers as soon as Sam was out of earshot. 'Here, you can do this one too. You're more suited to scrubbing than me. So tell me, what does Dan see in you?'

Eva scrubbed harder, pretending the plate was Rose's face.

'What I want to know is, how did Dan find you so quickly? He jilts me, then a few weeks later he's seeing you. There's something not right.' Rose narrowed her eyes, then she blinked and said conversationally, 'I went looking for him. Right after I heard from a friend that he was involved with you. You left in rather a hurry from the party. At first I thought you were going outside for some fresh air but I was relieved to see you weren't coming back. Then I cornered Daisy in the Ladies. She has no guile, does she? Found out Dan was coming on Bob's silly trip after all.' She snapped her fingers and Eva looked up. 'That's why he sponsored you, isn't it? So he could get out here and do his stuff on Harrap and keep Bob sweet by providing a translator instead of me. And you needed a ticket too for Bob's trip. I'm right, aren't I?'

'Yes, you're right.' Eva stacked the washed plates and slapped a mosquito off her arm. They were buzzing tonight in the warm air. No breeze to whisk them away. 'There's nothing between us — Dan's my sponsor, nothing more. I won't get in the way of whatever making up you and he have to do.' *Dan's welcome to you.* She didn't say it out loud.

'Glad to hear it,' Rose said sarcastically. She threw a small pebble, which went past Eva's ear and landed without a noise in the rushing water. 'It would never have worked out for you anyway. Dan likes a certain kind of woman. A real woman, one who's soft and malleable and likes being protected.'

'And that's you, is it?' Eva said, wishing she could swat Rose as simply as the mozzies.

Rose nodded. 'It's a version of me. And it's who Dan fell in love with.'

'Didn't he dump you?' Eva asked rudely.

'A misunderstanding,' Rose hissed, then calmed herself. She smoothed down her pale hair and flickered her eyelashes as if in confused femininity. 'He loves me and I love him. He's strong and commanding and masculine, everything I want in a man. And I will have him back.'

'Good luck with that then,' Eva said, thrusting the pile of sopping wet tin plates into Rose's arms, 'Here, you can carry these back up. Sam'll be impressed.'

Sam had the big pot and was whistling yet another of his vast repertoire of tunes. Rose quickly lost her sour face as he arrived. With a ladylike grace she led the way back to the glade. Eva grinned.

She wasn't grinning some time later when Dan cornered her in her tent. He was practically on top of her, his jaw was thrust so far forward in anger. 'What the hell did you think you were doing offering to go with Bob to the village? Do you enjoy danger?' His eyes glittered. 'Have you seen the injuries a machete can inflict?'

Eva shrank back, only to feel the canvas tent behind her. 'It's none of your business what I decide to do,' she said, more firmly than she felt.

'I am your . . . '

'My sponsor? So what. That doesn't give you the right to tell me what to do. Besides, I'm not your responsibility. We're simply team members.' Eva's voice was dripping with scorn.

'We know each other a little better than that, don't we,' Dan said silkily. She felt his warm breath, spicy from dinner, and the scent of his skin so familiar from their kissing. She shivered. In spite of his anger, she wanted to touch him right there and then. She half reached for him in blind instinct. He drew a finger slowly along her cheekbone and the tiny hairs on the back of her neck sprang up in anticipation. But he moved back abruptly and the spell was broken.

'What about Rose?' Eva couldn't help asking.

'She doesn't know what she's getting herself into,' Dan said, rubbing his jaw as if weary all of a sudden. 'Bob's a fool to take her.'

'Maybe she's tougher than you think,' Eva said.

'Doubtful,' he answered. 'She's not like you. She's delicate; she needs looking after.'

Eva snorted in a very unladylike fashion. Dan quirked an eyebrow. 'Well you'd better go and look after her then. Last I saw, she was struggling with her mosquito netting. Don't worry about me, I'll be fine here. I'll search my boots for snakes all by myself.'

'Don't be so childish, Eva.'

Eva ignored him and rolled over on her bed to face the wall. Behind her, Dan gave an exasperated sigh and stomped noisily out of her tent, leaving the zip open. Blast the man! She crawled over to the entrance to zip out the night and caught sight of him over at Rose's tent, unfurling netting and draping it. Rose had her hands adoringly at her cheeks, watching him. Eva zipped up violently.

It took an hour or two for the truth to sink in. When it did, she sat bolt upright in her bed. She didn't just like Dan. She liked him very, very much. The truth was, she was falling in love with him.

8

Eva understood why Dan had fallen in love with Rose. She was charming when she wanted to be. She put herself out to be entertaining and attentive on the journey. As long as she had the attention of all the males around her she was sweet as honey. In return, men protected her, made sure she was comfortable, didn't swear and generally acted like gentlemen. Eva tried to see it as animal behaviour. It was amusing to watch Bob carefully blow his cigar smoke away from Rose. Usually he blasted it out merrily in a foul fug to whoever was within range. James acted like Rose's lap dog, getting her whatever she mentioned and sitting beside her in the jeep to point out things of interest in the jungle.

Eva carried her new awareness of her love for Dan like a precious ball right in the centre of her heart. How had it come about? It had slipped in under the radar to hit her full impact. Wham. There was no way she'd tell him. It changed nothing. At the end of the trip they'd go their separate ways. If Rose had her way, Dan wouldn't be leaving alone. He was aloof today, driving the jeep along the crumbling road northeast from the camp up into the most remote parts of the island. He didn't respond to Rose's laughter and chat in the back, nor join in the banter which James was so good at rousing. Eva sat up front beside him, being jarred up and down with each pothole.

'How's the driving?' she asked him, to break his silence.

'Appalling,' he said briefly.

'Will it take us long to get there?' Already she felt nauseous from the constant motion of the jeep.

'This is wild country.' Dan glanced over at her, then back to the road. 'Very remote. These villages are not like the ones we drove through from Galanga.

The people up here don't make contact with the outside world if they can help it. Don't need to. The jungle provides for them. So yes, it'll take us a while to get up there.'

'You're still mad we're going, aren't you?'

Dan sighed. 'I think it's crazy, yes. Whatever stirred up the chiefs, my guess is it won't have gone away in these few days. God knows what kind of reception we're going to get.'

'So why come along?'

'Because I'm not going to let you walk into danger without me.'

A strange happiness filled her — which was weird, because she should be frightened of what awaited them. *I'm not going to let you walk into danger without me.* Did he mean her particularly? Or did 'you' encompass the whole group? It didn't matter. What mattered was having Dan with her.

They were all hot and tired by the time the jeep stopped, hours later. The decision was taken to make camp and take the opportunity to collect specimens. Then the next day they'd go to the villages.

'With the hope that an extra day will have calmed the chiefs,' Bob said with his usual ponderous humour. 'Anyone join me for a swim? Get rid of the grime.'

They were on the northeast coast. The view was that of paradise: golden sand untouched by footprints, palm trees, small outcrops of rock topped with exotic flowered plants, and always, always the turquoise ocean. Eva was reminded of Maracca Bay. She looked over at Dan. Was he remembering it too? But he was deep in conversation with Rose and Eva's happiness fled. Did he still love Rose? Was he regretting jilting her?

'What are they so cosy about?' James said to Eva. There was a jealous edge to his voice.

She shrugged and turned away, pretending to rummage in her kit bag. She'd no intention of getting involved in Rose's emotional spiderweb.

But that was impossible. Especially when Rose emerged from behind a discreet palm clad only in a skimpy hot pink bikini. James's adam's apple bobbed in his throat. Bob cleared his throat with a rumbling cough. Dan's expression was unreadable. He continued unloading the jeep as Rose whispered to him on her way past, hips swaying, down the beach to the sea edge.

'Who's joining me?' she called. 'The water's warm.'

In the end they all swam, in lieu of showers. It was better to be clean and sticky with salt water than sweaty and dust-streaked. Eva then took on the cooking duties. Trying to copy Daisy, she boiled up water, added a purifier and some vegetables, and made a kind of soup. She ladled a spoonful out and stared at it doubtfully.

'Fill it up,' Bob barked cheerfully, brandishing his tin bowl. His hair was an Einstein shock, stiff with salt. 'Very good,' he added after a gulp and winked at her.

The others were eating, too, with no complaints. Rose picked at hers, leaving a little row of carrot slices alone. She sipped daintily at the remaining liquid.

'You should eat up,' Dan told her. 'Long walk tomorrow.'

'I have a light appetite, you know that darling.' Rose touched his arm.

Eva stirred the soup furiously. Daisy had let slip a few facts that morning about Dan and Rose. Eva had encouraged her brazenly, helping cook breakfast while Daisy chatted. It turned out Dan had fallen in love with Rose at first sight. They'd met at a university function a year ago and were engaged within weeks. A whirlwind romance, Daisy said. But when Eva asked why it had all gone wrong, Daisy refused to say. On that alone, she couldn't be drawn.

But later that night, Eva was pretty certain she knew the answer. The question was, how forgiving was Dan?

The rows of specimen jars were lined

up on a piece of tarpaulin, ready to be boxed in the morning. The nets and pooters lay scattered next to them. Night had fallen and they were all rolled up in sleeping bags around the fire. The insects weren't so bad. Perhaps the coastal breeze kept them away. Eva was restless. She couldn't sleep. Bob seemed happy with her, but when he read Gwendolin's letter that would all change. She couldn't bear it. She was fitting in to the team. She was doing her best. Her mother was about to undermine all her hard work.

A rustling noise startled her. She must've drifted into sleep after all, because now she was wide awake and alert. Images of hostile natives or large jungle cats froze her to the spot. The jungle was black. The fire had long ago died down to ashes. Cautiously, she craned her neck up. Just a little. Not wanting to draw attention to her movement. A shadowy figure was tiptoeing *into* the camp. Eva screwed up her eyes to focus better. She saw a slim outline and long flowing hair. It was Rose. She was acting strangely. Staring around her jumpily and then slipping into her bag fast. Eva was about to lie down again when she heard the crack of a branch. Someone else was awake and up. Then she saw him. James. Moving furtively to the far side of the fire and then lying down still. If anyone woke now they'd see nothing suspicious. Rose and James. Poor Christa. And poor Dan. Had Rose cheated on him before? Was that why he'd dumped her so abruptly?

The next morning, Eva began to doubt her own senses. There was no special body language between Rose and James. Rose was flirting with all three men as she'd done before. It was as natural to her as talking. They packed up the jeep with what they were leaving behind and hoisted on their rucksacks. Now they were to hike the coastal trail until they reached the villages. It was a glorious dry day, although black clouds out at sea threatened a tropical downpour later. The path was narrow but visible. Bob led, then in line they followed with James, then Rose, then Eva and Dan at the rear. She was comforted by that. Dan wouldn't let her fall behind if she was slower. Although she needn't worry on that score. Rose was much slower than her. Eva was constantly brought up short. Once she trod accidentally on Rose's heel, earning an exaggerated scream.

'What size feet do you have? Keep them away from me.'

'Sorry,' Eva said apologetically. 'If you could speed up a bit.'

'Don't blame me!' Rose snapped. Then she collected herself. Nice Rose back in place. 'It's okay. I'll have a blister now but I'll manage.' She tossed her hair and tottered on. She walked as if she had high heels on despite wearing brand-new hiking boots.

Out at sea the frigate birds sailed the thermals. On the beach, a herd of quenks squealed and quarrelled over fallen coconuts. On their right-hand side the foliage brushed them, laced with heavy waxy flowers, and the occasional colourful parrot flew up squawking. Eva hummed one of Sam's melodies. It was that kind of day. There was a pace and rhythm to the walking which was hypnotic once she avoided Rose's feet. Bob was shouting back advice for when they encountered the locals but she couldn't hear him. It didn't matter right then. It was so peaceful. She couldn't imagine it otherwise. She wanted to spend the rest of her life here.

It was James who triggered the tripwire. And James who paid the price. They had paused to admire the scenery and catch their breath. Off the main track which they were following there were other fainter paths radiating off in amongst the tree trunks. Eva wiped her brow and took a drink from her water bottle. Rose sat on her rucksack, fanning her face with a real silk fan produced from her pack. Bob and Dan were arguing over a map. James pointed into the forest.

'Hey, there's oranges. Who fancies a juicy orange for lunch? Rose?'

'James — we should stick to the path,' Dan warned, hearing him.

Rose shook her head, making sure her hair fell becomingly over her shoulders. 'Oh don't be silly. What's the problem? Personally, I'd *love* a fresh orange. James? Going to get me one?'

'No probs. Anyone else?'

Dan's mouth tightened but he turned back to Bob who was waving the map and telling him something.

James walked into the forest on a faint trail. Seconds later there was a loud crack of gunshot and a chilling silence, then screaming. Eva ran after Dan into the jungle. She almost tripped over a shoe. When she looked down her heart stopped. It was blood-splattered. Dan had reached James. He was deathly white and unconscious. Horrified, Eva saw that his lower left leg was very badly injured. The screaming went on and on. It wasn't James any more; it was Rose.

'Eva, get my bag. We have to stop the blood loss,' Dan said quietly. 'Rose, help me with James. We must move him in case of more traps.'

'No, no, no!' Rose backed away, shaking, 'I'm not touching him. There's blood . . . everywhere.'

Eva swiftly got the medical kit and handed it to Dan. Then she gently lifted James, with Bob helping. They moved him to the main path, leaving a heavy trail of blood. Rose stood shivering and crying. They ignored her, intent on saving James's life. Dan gave instructions calmly and Eva did what he asked.

Bob went along the path with the handset, hoping for a signal. He came back shaking his head. 'It's no use. It's dead. We'll have to carry him out.'

'What!' Rose shrieked, 'And how do you propose we do that? It's taken us hours to get this far. We should get help from the village.'

Dan and Eva exchanged looks. James was going to die without hospital treatment. Eva was no medic, but it didn't take a doctor to see he was in a bad way. Rose's hysteria was helping no one. 'We'll make a stretcher,' Eva suggested. 'Rose, come and help me. We'll take the machetes and cut branches.'

Rose refused point blank. 'I can't do that. I'm not strong enough.' She sat down and curled her arms round herself.

Bob took a machete and gave the other to Eva. They hacked and sliced at the plants until they had a bundle of branches to lash together with lengths of tough vine. Eva was panting with exertion. The humidity was intense.

She crouched down next to James. His forehead was beaded with drops of moisture but his skin was waxy. Dan had tourniqueted his leg but the bandages were stained crimson like rose blossoms.

'What happened to him?' Eva asked.

'Booby traps,' Dan said grimly. 'I

should've known. I should've stopped him. This area is notorious for drug baron territories. If one ventures off the main track, there are trip wires and sawn-off shotguns waiting to be triggered. I never thought . . . '

Eva reached for him. She hugged him fiercely. There was a pause, then he was holding her so tightly that it hurt. But she let him. Then he dropped his arms.

'I've made him as comfortable as possible. But we have to get out of here. It's his only chance.'

Bob finished tying the last join in the makeshift stretcher. 'Now we know why the chief was so angry. They've had problems with drug barons moving them out of their lands before. I bet they've been threatened.'

'You take Rose and get to the village,' Dan said, making a sudden decision. 'She can talk to the chief. There might be a phone or a runner who could get help to us. Eva and I will stretcher James as far as we can towards the jeep. If we get there, we'll drive south. There's

a small hospital run by nuns in Verive.'
He named a town midway between the
northern coast and Galanga.

'I don't want to go,' Rose wailed.
'What if the drug guys are there? We
might get killed.'

'Do you want to lift James instead?'
Dan said, his voice pure steel.

Rose took a wavering look at James's
messed-up leg and burst into fresh
tears.

'Right, let's get going,' Bob said with
forced cheerfulness. 'Good luck, you
two.'

Eva saw him as an old man in that
instant. He was in his mid-seventies.
His hand shook ever so slightly on the
haft of the machete. Either a tremor of
old age or suppressed fear. She felt a
rush of tenderness for him. Funny how
she wasn't afraid of him anymore, nor
daunted by his view of her. However he
reacted to what Gwendolin had to tell
him, she didn't care. It was nothing to
what they were going through right
now.

Sniffling, Rose refused the other machete so Bob carried them both. Gently and firmly, he guided Rose onto the track with a hand between the shoulder blades. No going back. Eva prayed they'd get a good reception from the chief.

The stretcher was shockingly heavy. Eva's shoulders and arms ached instantly from James's slack weight. She knew Dan had given her the easier end to carry. He tried to take the bulk of the weight at the head end. They walked in silence for a while, concentrating on their footsteps and breathing.

'You mustn't blame her,' Eva said softly, sometime later when they took a brief rest to gather their strength. 'You said it yourself, she's delicate.'

Why on earth she felt she had to defend Rose, she didn't know. She'd liked James enough to flirt with him and meet him clandestinely last night. But she'd run from helping him today. But Eva couldn't bear Dan's unhappiness. If it was Rose he loved, then he must be concerned about her.

'She should never have come to Trinita,' Dan said feelingly. 'It's a wild place. It's not London or Hawaii. There are dangers. We've seen that now.'

'I've never been so scared in all my life,' Eva admitted. James moaned in his comatose state and she felt his forehead. It was burning up. 'We should go. He's feverish,' Eva said, even though Dan was the doctor and the one who should be diagnosing.

'Eva, wait.' Dan's tawny eyes gazed straight into her own, as if he looked right inside her and saw her very soul. 'I'm proud of you today. I want you to know that.'

Eva burned up with pride. It gave her strength to lift the stretcher and carry on. Dan's approval lit her up inside. It wasn't a profession of undying love but it was the next best thing.

The hours that followed were forever jumbled up in her mind. The searing pain in her muscles, the unyielding ground, one foot after another until her body screamed. Fearing they would never find the jeep. Then the awful drive back down winding, eroded roads with cliff edges. The rain began: great black sheets of it pounding on the jeep's roof and sliding off the windscreen. The ancient wipers, fringed in shredded rubber, making no impact on the water pouring off the glass. Stopping when they couldn't see the road. James moaning. Worse, James so silent that Eva had to lean over to feel his faint breath on her cheek. He clung to life as they bumped and jolted their way to Verive. The muffled rasp of the nuns' long capes as they took him into the hospital. The thunderous roar and battle of the rain on the corrugated metal. Mud and blood smeared on Eva's clothes, on her face. And always Dan. Every step of the way.

They stayed overnight in a small house in the hospital grounds. Eva didn't know who it belonged to, perhaps one of the nursing staff, but there was a hot shower and clean clothes laid out for them. A vehicle had been sent to pick up Bob and Rose. It intercepted them on the road where they were being driven south by the Crab Man. The next day they all met again in the hospital kitchen.

'The Crab Man is a character known by everyone in the villages,' Bob explained. He was shovelling cereal as if he'd never tasted it before. He wiped his mouth apologetically and went on, 'We reached the village late in the afternoon. They weren't pleased to see us. Threatened us with rather unpleasant consequences if we came in.' He glanced at Rose, who was sitting sullenly, picking at a small slice of toast.

'Rose was able to speak to the chief in his own language and explain what had happened to James. Turns out you were right, Dan. They've had big trouble with drug lords pushing into their lands and trying to force them out. So far they're resisting. But who knows . . . village knives against sophisticated guns.' He shook his head glumly and poured another bowl of cereal and milk.

'And the Crab Man?' Dan prompted. He looked fresh and energised compared to the rest of them, Eva thought. She felt battered and bruised and could've done with a hairbrush and a touch of moisturiser. Her skin was raw from the sun and rain and insect bites. Rose was clearly suffering similarly. Her hair was tangled and there were two red patches, one on each cheek, like badly applied rouge.

'The Crab Man lives in a tumbledown hut on the coast. He catches crabs and sells them to the villagers. No one knows much about his history but he has an ancient car and a radio set. Mysterious but rather helpful, given the circumstances.' Bob laughed at his own joke.

Rose wrinkled her nose and dropped the toast back onto the plate. 'Disgusting bread. I want to go home. Why can't we leave now?' She folded her arms and looked sour.

'Come along, my dear. You've done so well so far. We'll be home soon,' Bob said gallantly. He helped himself to Rose's discarded toast and ate it with relish.

'Home?' Rose snarled. 'You can't mean that smelly campsite? I mean *really* home. Where there's hot water, shampoo and my manicurist on tap.'

'You'll wish to visit James on the ward before we go,' Dan said. It wasn't a question. It was a reprimand.

Rose didn't even have the grace to blush. 'How is he?' she asked reluctantly.

'I'm going to say goodbye now. You can come with me,' Eva said, rising from the table.

The ward smelt of antiseptic and paint. There was an open window and in the courtyard outside, a man was painting the tree trunks white against termites. James lay in a metal bed with plastic tubes attached to his arm and nose. He was sleeping peacefully. His leg was well bandaged. Thankfully, the doctors had managed to save his leg, but he was going to need care and recuperation. Eva wondered if Christa would cope. If she stayed with him. What if she found out about him and Rose?

Eva turned fiercely to Rose. 'You mustn't tell her. Promise me.'

Rose was wafting air under her nose and looking ill. She didn't pretend to misunderstand. 'So you saw us. I thought you did. It didn't mean anything. It was a bit of fun. Goodness, the last thing I'd want is James leaving his wife for me. Hideous thought.' She shivered dramatically.

'Was that before or after he almost lost his leg?' Eva asked sharply.

Now Rose blushed. 'I'm out of here. I can't stand hospitals, they give me the heebie jeebies. And it stinks. Dan will take me home.'

9

Dan was angry. He was angry with Bob for blundering on with the trip to the villages in spite of his advice. He was angry with James for leaving the path. He was angry with Rose for what she had done. But mostly, he was angry with himself. And so he did what he always did when confused or in turmoil. He worked. There was no way into the northern isolated villages now to study Harrap, but he set up a clinic in Verive to treat minor ailments and diagnose more serious conditions. Then he directed his patients to the nuns' hospital. Being in Verive was a break from the tensions in the camp too. Rose was at loggerheads with her own team. She wanted to go home but they wanted to stay for the reasons they'd come in the first place. Eva wasn't happy either. Bob had called her into his tent. There was a letter apparently that needed discussing. When Eva emerged, her jaw was gripped and she wouldn't talk about it to anyone.

Dan couldn't stop thinking about her. She'd clung to him the night they'd reached the Verive Hospital. In the strange little house he'd kissed her passionately and stroked her damp hair from her face. It was the giving and taking of comfort after their ordeal, but Dan realised it was no longer simply a physical longing he had for Eva. It was no light love affair from which he might leave with his heart intact. He was falling in love with her. Hence his anger. His heart and soul were at risk. After Rose, he'd no intention of letting that happen again. He pushed his feelings down. He'd rather live his life alone than suffer another betrayal of trust.

As for Rose . . . If he'd wanted resolution, he most definitely had it. The journey to the villages and the crisis over James had opened his eyes to her failings. A quite different Rose had appeared under pressure. But the clincher had been the night assignation between her and James. He'd been awake, unable to rest. He saw first Rose, then James return to the fire. It was sad but unsurprising. No shock there for him. Any ember of his love for her had died that night.

So here he was, alone and working all hours to exhaustion point. After a week he had a phone call from Bob. 'We need our camp doctor back, Dan. I'm not averse to you running your clinic but we've a few conditions here that could do with your perusal. When can you get back?'

'Another twenty-four hours,' Dan said. 'I can't just leave. Anything serious?'

'Don't know,' Bob admitted. 'Billy's coral cuts aren't healing. Gail's complaining about her rash, says you didn't treat it properly. I don't believe that, by the way. Sam's knocked a lump out of his finger cutting wood. And Eva . . . '

'What's wrong with Eva?' His heart fluttered in fear. 'Bob?'

'I'm still here, crackly line, sorry. It may be nothing but . . . she's subdued. Unlike her. Goes to bed early and sleeps late. Bit unsociable, to tell the truth. Daisy's upset with her, commented on it to me.' There was a loud sigh from Bob's end of the line. 'This expedition is turning out to be more bother than I'd planned for. Christa's distracted, she won't climb and she's got flight tickets home.'

'James can't fly home with his leg like that,' Dan protested.

'She's not waiting for him. Whole thing's a mess. Big blow-up between her and Rose yesterday. I have to say, I'm beginning to think you were right not to marry that girl, Dan. She's volatile. Manages to stir everyone up at each other.'

'Look, I'll come as soon as I can,' Dan promised. 'There's a bus late tomorrow. I'll get on it and walk when I have to. If you can meet me with the jeep, great.' He worked solidly until then but all he could think of was Eva. What was wrong with her? Suddenly he couldn't wait to be back in the northern ranges at their campsite.

★ ★ ★

Eva was listless. She couldn't shake it off. She wanted to sleep, and when she wasn't sleeping she wished to doze. She put it down to a delayed reaction to James's accident. She struggled in the morning to get her stuff together for her studies. Bob had finally received Gwendolin's letter. He called her in to talk about it a few days after they returned to camp.

'I want to know if you're coping, that's all,' he blustered when Eva accused him of taking her mother's side. 'Your welfare is important, as are the study results. Can you manage?'

'Is that a genuine concern?' Eva said hotly, 'or a veiled threat?'

'Now listen, young lady,' Bob began, but she interrupted him.

'No, you listen, Bob. Instead of reading about stuff that happened a long, long time ago, why don't you go by what I'm doing now? I grew up. My mother . . . Gwendolin . . . won't accept that. Doesn't see it. But I'm here and I'm doing the work and I am confident that I'll get a good paper out of it that you can be proud to put your name on along with mine.' She felt good when it all came rolling off her tongue. She'd never imagined speaking to Professor Grierson so bluntly. But although she still respected him, somehow he didn't scare her anymore. What scared her was quite different. Shotguns wounding people. Chaotic violence when least expected. And, at the opposite end of the scale — love. It scared her how much she was in love with Dan. How much she was going to miss him when he went to Verive. How she couldn't tell him her feelings for him. Not while Rose was on the scene.

Not while she suspected he might still be in love with his ex-fiancée.

Bob put up his hands in mock surrender. 'Okay, point taken. I have every respect for your mother's views but I do agree you appear to be doing a good job. I'll say no more. Let's see that draft paper soon, eh?' He winked and shooed her out of the tent with no resentment. Eva was relieved. She'd crossed a line, she knew. She was lucky to get away with it.

Then Dan left and she was hollow without him. Rose and Christa had a huge argument. Someone had let the cat out of the bag. Rose was left with a long scratch down her face where Christa had clawed her in fury. You could never tell what people were capable of, Eva mused. And that included her. She was finally over Connecticut. She'd survived Gwendolin's revelations to Bob and come out fighting. But now she was tired, so tired. She couldn't bear to sit with the others round the fire at night. She was too aware of Dan's empty space and Rose's little comments and her energy was leached from her by teatime anyway. It was so obvious that Daisy had accused her of being anti-social. That was hurtful coming from a woman she considered a friend, and Eva shut herself away even more.

She was glad when Bob asked her to visit the divers at the coast. She took letters and food and Bob asked her to take photographs for the blog diary. It was an excuse, they both knew it, but she grabbed the excuse gratefully. A day at the beach might be the tonic she needed. Wandering along the pristine white sands, she felt peaceful, hypnotic as the waves were. She took loads of photos of the beach and of the divers getting ready for another day under the surface of the sea. She watched as they waded into the water and one by one disappeared. More snaps of bubbles rising, an occasional flipper rising like a shark fin and, once, Ann's hand gripping a blue starfish for the camera.

Once she had enough, she went back up to the house. Dan was sitting in the wicker chair by the window. He stood when he saw her and frowned.

'Nice to see you too,' Eva said. Her heart was pounding so hard she was amazed he didn't comment on the sound. Did he have to give her such a black look?

Dan tried for a smile. 'Sorry. I am pleased to see you. Bob asked me to check on you. He said you weren't well?'

'I'm not ill, just tired.' Eva turned to look out the window. Someone, Billy or Brian maybe, was way out at the far edge of the coral. A black blurred shape under the turquoise sheen, looking like a predator.

'Let me check you over anyway,' Dan suggested. He took her wrist and counted her pulse. It jumped at his touch. He shone a light into her eyes, pressed her fingernails for colour and checked her breathing. 'Nothing particular stands out,' he said finally, 'But let's keep an eye on you. Fatigue is a general symptom of too many conditions. Or it could be nothing at all.' He paused, looking at her closely. 'You're a little flushed. No temperature, but tell me if you start to feel worse.'

If she was flushed, it was because of his proximity. Okay, he was simply doing his job, but his touch and nearness were almost too much for her. She sensed though that something had changed between them. There was a reserve to Dan that hadn't been there before. James's accident had changed things. Dan had run off to Verive. Why? Rose had hinted she was going there too. Had he planned for that? With despair, Eva reminded herself that Dan wasn't truly free. If he was, would she confess her love for him? It was all too complicated. No wonder she was tired. She had to concentrate on her paper for Bob.

There was a silence. Dan re-packed his medical bag. Eva arranged seashells on the windowsill. Then he snapped his fingers as if finding a solution. 'Fancy a visit to someone who makes a proper cup of English tea?'

'Okay. Bit random, but why not.'

'Let's go. I'll catch up with Billy and Gail later for their medicines.'

The bungalow was low and sprawling, freshly painted and shaded by deep pink bougainvillea blossoms. A lemon tree, heavy with fruit, stood like a slender lady in the driveway. Along the street were similar bungalows, all well tended, neat and colourful. There was a wide wooden verandah running the length of the front of the house. On it was a rocking chair, and in the chair sat an old woman. At their approach she slowly rose on shaky limbs.

'Hallo. Welcome, welcome.' Her coffee-and-cream complexion was criss-crossed with a map of wrinkles, but her eyes were bright and twinkling. She seized Dan round the waist and squeezed him. She was about half his height. Eva had never seen such a tiny old woman.

'My grandson.' A throaty chuckle and another fond squeeze of Dan's ribs.

He kissed the top of her kerchiefed head. 'Angelica, can I introduce you to Eva?'

The old lady took both of Eva's hands in hers and stared straight up into her eyes. Eva felt the rough calluses of fingers that had worked hard. Whatever she saw satisfied her, for she nodded; and, still holding Eva's hand, took her into the coolness of the house.

Inside was just as neat and clean as the exterior. It was sparsely furnished in the main room, a couch and armchairs and a coffee table. One glass-fronted cabinet contained a collection of china, and framed photographs were displayed on the waxed top. She left them sitting on the couch while she went into another room and Eva heard the clink of porcelain and the hiss of a running tap.

'You never told me your gran was from Trinita.' It came out sounding like an accusation.

Dan quirked an eyebrow at her. 'It's no secret. You and I don't know each other very well. There's lots of things you don't know about me, and I'm pretty sure there are things about you that I don't know.'

She thought of the letter and Bob's summons to his tent. She hadn't wanted to tell Dan anything; she was too embarrassed and angry at the time. But she guessed that was what he was referring to. The fact was, they knew each other's bodies more intimately than each other's minds.

She flushed as she glanced at him. He was thinking the same thing, she could tell. A slow smile curved his lip and his gaze lingered on her mouth. A tension rose between them, sweet and delicious, swirling like smoke in heat. Then Angelica arrived with a tray of tea and scones, and the moment was broken.

Eva noticed then that the backs of the woman's hands and her forearms were covered in raised pink lesions.

Healed rather than open. Harrap virus. It explained Dan's passion for finding a cure. As she followed that line of thought, she was struck by another. But then Angelica was talking, asking her how she liked the island and the people, and she was answering. Still, it ticked away at the back of her mind, simmering.

'You looking after my boy?' Angelica beamed, touching Dan's hair proudly. 'He fierce like the tiger but inside, just so soft like a ripe mango. He do anything for you, I know it.'

'Oh, it's not like that,' Eva said quickly, 'We're not . . .'

'You together, I can tell it,' the old woman said firmly. 'You look after him right.'

Dan grinned. 'Gran knows about voodoo so don't argue with her, Eva.'

Angelica chuckled. It was a rich, throaty sound. 'Silly boy. Now tell me, why you say your fiancée have yellow hair and big blue eyes? You colour blind now?'

Eva drew a breath in. Outside, a couple of blue macaws squabbled in a passion fruit vine high up on the yard wall. Dan stood up and stared out the window at the birds. Then he turned back and sat again, pouring tea into the three cups, although no one had asked. 'I didn't get time to write to you about Rose. It didn't work out. There were . . . issues between us. Eva and I . . . well, we're friends, that's it.'

Angelica narrowed her eyes and gave him a shrewd stare. Dan shook his head. He wasn't going to say more. Eva tried to interpret what he meant. How he felt about Rose. It was impossible. Rose's behaviour had been appalling in the aftermath of the accident, but then Dan had missed most of it by running off to Verive. Why had he done that? What was he running from? Sadly, she realised that in a few short weeks they'd return to England and go their separate ways. Then Dan and Rose could sort out their issues and get back together.

That flickering thought had simmered to boiling point. Dan didn't need to sweeten Bob Grierson to get to the jungle villages. His own grandmother was an islander. She would know who to contact and how to go about it. She probably spoke the language too. Which meant that Dan hadn't sponsored Eva as a ticket to Bob's expedition. He'd sponsored her to punish Rose. Pure and simple. He was in love with Rose. Weren't love and hate two sides of the same coin? If he didn't care about Rose so intensely, then he wouldn't have meted out such a terrible revenge.

Eva's tiredness returned like a weighted blanket, dropping down over her head to muffle her from the world. They finished their tea, Dan and Angelica swapping stories while Eva mouthed politely whatever was needed to show she was fine, she was there and there was no need to worry. Soon after, they made their goodbyes and Dan drove them back to camp.

Eva leaned her head on the cool glass of the door's window. She was sick with fatigue and love and despair. As they swung the jeep onto the turning circle, she saw Rose and her team walking out of the jungle. Rose brightened at the sight of Dan and stopped. One of her team said something and she scowled. She looked like she'd argue with him but followed the others with shoulders stiff with outrage. They were out of sight by the time Eva and Dan descended from the vehicle, ready to hike the trail.

'That's a shame, you missed speaking with her,' Eva forced herself to say. It was like twisting a knife into her stomach. Rose and Dan. Dan and Rose. She had to forget how she felt about Dan or go mad.

'She'll catch me later,' Dan said enigmatically.

The trail was fainter and much thicker with vegetation that had grown fast, knitting together over the gap. Or else why did she stumble along on feet that felt like they were encased in cement? What was wrong with her?

They halted to let a stream of army ants pour across the path. On the surface of the bobbing, seething mass, a large paralysed caterpillar was being passed, conveyor-belt-efficient. Eva was like the caterpillar. Trapped and powerless. Being taken by events to goodness knew where.

When they got back to the camp, Daisy ran forward to give her a hug. A sign she was forgiven her shunning of the fire. It put a stop to Eva's maudlin ideas and she returned it, glad to see her friend. Sam was there too, and even Christa turned out of her tent to greet them. Eva's spirits lifted. It would be okay. All she had to do was finish her research and curb her emotions. She vowed to treat Dan as a friend and nothing more. They'd taken pleasure and comfort in each other but it had to stop. Dan and Rose must be given time and space to work things out. Eva wouldn't get in their way.

With this new resolve, she went into her tent. There was a postcard for her on her sleeping bag. On one side was an iconic image of Big Ben and the Houses of Parliament illuminated at night. On the other side, one scrawled sentence. Gwendolin was arriving the next day.

10

Gwendolin proceeded to take charge on arrival. The jeep arrived back from the airport in the early afternoon, having taken Christa there and Gwendolin back with it, and she alighted from the jungle path with a spring in her step. Eva was lying on her bed, feeling alternately hot and cold and shivery. She heard her mother's crisp tones, questioning, and Bob's deep gruff answer. Her heart sank. She dragged herself upright and tried to brush her hair. Her arm was weak and the brush felt incredibly heavy. If she didn't hurry, though, she could quite imagine Gwendolin pushing her way into the tent and berating her for sleeping in the daytime.

'Gwendolin, you made it. Good journey?' Eva managed a smile as she went to greet her.

Her mother was dressed for action in

a crisp linen tropical suit and khaki sunhat. It suited her. 'Goodness, you look awful. What's wrong with you? That expedition doctor not looking after you? Bob, why didn't you tell me Eva was ill?'

Bob seemed unduly cowed. Given how much he went on about Eva's mother and what a great scientist she was, maybe he was awed at being in his heroine's presence. Eva turned a little laugh into a cough. Once started, it became a real cough.

'I had no idea she was so bad,' Bob blustered. 'Eva, you should've told me you weren't well.'

So now it was all her own fault. Gwendolin had managed it once again. She always wrong-footed Eva, twisting things round so it looked like she couldn't cope. It was probably unintentional but had become a habit over the years. Was that how her mother really saw her? As a person who basically couldn't sort her own life out? Connecticut echoing through the years again.

'I'm fine, really,' Eva said, more sharply than she intended.

Gwendolin raised her eyebrows. 'No need to be snappy, darling. I only want what's best for you. Perhaps you should rest.' Bob was nodding in agreement behind her.

'I'm fine,' Eva repeated firmly. 'Let me help you get your stuff.'

'Oh don't worry about that. Bob's got it under control. Now, if you won't rest, then you can take me on a tour of the camp.'

Bob shuffled off to unpack and Gwendolin hooked her arm in Eva's and steered her in the direction of the campfire.

'Why did you come? Haven't you got too much work at home?' Eva asked as Gwendolin stuck a toe in the fire ashes and examined them.

'For you. I came for you,' Gwendolin said in surprise, as if it were obvious. 'You need me. Besides, I need a break from endless marking. I may as well have a short holiday here and enjoy the wildlife. I can help you do your research too.'

'And Bob let you come out here. Just like that?'

'I bullied him into it. Bob's precious about his little expeditions. But I can be very persuasive,' Gwendolin laughed.

Eva glanced over to the far side of the camp where Bob was busy putting up an extra tent. Gwendolin's bags lay on the ground beside him. That was one good thing about her mother, she travelled light.

They walked down to the river's edge and away from everyone. Eva wondered how Dan was getting on in Verive. He'd gone again early that morning despite Bob's grumbles that he was needed here. 'I didn't realise you knew Bob that well.' Eva cooled her feet in the fast-flowing water.

'I've known him for years. Same research circles, that sort of thing. Oh look!' Gwendolin pointed to a bright green parrot in a tree. Eva got the distinct impression her mother was evading her question but she let it pass for now.

'How's camp life?' Gwendolin asked stiffly when Eva offered no comment on the parrot. 'Have you had enough yet? Dan turned out to be everything you thought, or has he turned out to be a mere mortal after all?'

'You're so bitter about your own failed marriage,' Eva said, shaking her head in exasperation. 'Not everyone else's relationship turns out like that. Besides, he and I aren't involved, we're simply friends.'

Dan hadn't let her down. Not in the ways that mattered. He'd saved her from drowning in the oil bird caves. He'd been with her all the way mentally and physically in the race to save James's life. The only way he'd failed her was in not loving her with the same strong passion and fervour with which she loved him. He belonged to Rose. It was like a dagger to the heart to think about it. She forced her mind away and onto Gwendolin who was answering her in the same stiff tone.

'You hardly knew him when you announced to me you were getting him to sponsor your travels here. I couldn't understand it at all. At first I put it down to your unpredictability, which you inherited from your father. Then, later, I realised what it was. You were running away. Again. You escaped out here to Trinita to avoid finishing your doctorate. Didn't you?'

'I wasn't running away or escaping!' Eva said angrily. What was it about Gwendolin that got her so riled? She had a knack of getting right under Eva's skin. 'I needed to get on this expedition. I wanted to do something *good*. To be the best student Bob had ever had. To prove to you, Gwendolin, that I could achieve it. Believe it or not, I actually came here to help me finish my doctorate. I want to add some extra results to it to back up my theories.' She flung a rock into the river, where it sent up a spray of brown water and sent a flock of grackles scattering from the bushes.

'To prove to me? Why?' Gwendolin seemed genuinely puzzled. Her hat was slightly askew, giving a mildly comical air to her that was at odds with the rest of her neat tropical outfit. It gave Eva a pang of tenderness. Why was she always at loggerheads with her mother?

'Why did you send that letter to Bob about Connecticut?' she countered with her own question, which had burned in her for days. 'I was doing so well, and then Bob read it and started doubting me.'

Gwendolin grimaced. 'That wasn't my intention. The opposite in fact. I wanted to caution Bob not to expect too much from you. I was trying to make it easier for you.'

'Easier! By telling him that I'm not good enough. I can't even begin to understand how you thought that would help.' Tears stung her eyes and she wiped them away angrily.

'I'm sorry,' Gwendolin said, removing her awful hat and pushing her hair away from a damp forehead abstractedly. 'I . . . I'm not good at the

Mum-and-daughter stuff. You know that, Eva. I was never one for sitting at the end of your bed listening to your teenage woes and talking through your emotional needs.'

Eva laughed harshly. There was no joy in the sound. She remembered clearly storming home from school one day in floods of tears because her best friend had dumped her for a circle of 'cool' girls. She'd barricaded herself in her bedroom and cried. Secretly, she'd hoped that her mother would insist on coming in and finding out what was wrong with her. Then she would let it all come out and her mother would help her find a solution and comfort her and tell her it didn't matter because she loved her and together they'd fight the world.

None of that happened. Gwendolin had simply worked on in her study and later called Eva down for supper without asking what the matter was. Eva was too stubborn to be first to say anything and a silent dinner had ensued with Eva eating with reddened, swollen eyes and a box of tissues while Gwendolin ate and made notes on a scientific paper at the same time.

'What I am good at is the intellectual side of things,' Gwendolin went on, sounding more confident. 'I know I can help you there. I want you to succeed and to be happy. If I can lend some support to that, then I will.'

'But the letter? It didn't help,' Eva said bluntly. 'You don't seem to realize that I've grown up. I can carry out responsibilities without running away. And not only that, but I've got a great research paper from my work here in Trinita and I don't need you butting in on that. I'm afraid you've had a wasted journey.' She turned on her heel and left Gwendolin there by the river.

*   *   *

Eva was building up wood for the evening's fire unnecessarily when Daisy caught up with her. 'Hey, leave that.

We're heading over to the coast to visit the divers. Are you coming?' Daisy's gaze was sympathetic, as if she could read Eva's mood.

'Sure, why not. I'll get my bag.' She was glad to get away from the camp and her own brooding thoughts. What she hadn't bargained on was that her mother and Bob were coming too. Eva was ready to turn back when she saw them waiting for her expectantly. She could blame her fatigue, say she felt ill and couldn't go. But it was too late. Daisy was beckoning her on impatiently.

'Come on. I want to get these supplies over to Ann today. Can you carry this, please?' Daisy handed Eva a sling bag of dehydrated packet meals that had been brought down in the jeep along with Gwendolin that day. She had no option but to take the bag and follow her mother along the route to the divers' huts.

There was no one in the huts. The divers' boat could be seen bobbing lazily offshore and they could make out snorkels near it. Bob offered to show Gwendolin the species of shells on the beach. Daisy was busy opening the meagre cupboards and storing the supplies. Eva wandered outside. Bob and her mother were talking animatedly as they went down to the shore. Probably arguing about obscure Latin names for the shells. A crunching sound of feet on coral sand made her turn. Rose was there, dressed in a pale lemon sundress and looking as fresh and cool as a holiday-maker. The look on her face said she hadn't expected to see Eva. Her nose wrinkled.

'What are you doing here?'

'Bringing food for the divers. And you?' Not that she cared. She hoped Rose would go away.

Rose shrugged carelessly. 'Wasting time. The others are writing up results and planning our next outing. I've done the translations, so they don't need me just now. I've come visiting.'

'There's no one home,' Eva told her.

'Who's that on the beach?' Rose asked, looking to where Gwendolin was peering into a rock pool while Bob showed her some small thing.

'My mother,' Eva admitted reluctantly.

'Your *mother*?' Rose sneered. 'You brought your mother along? What kind of baby are you? I must introduce myself. This will be interesting.' Before Eva could stop her, Rose half-ran past her and down to the beach. Eva went after her, fuming.

Rose had already exchanged names and handshakes when Eva caught up. Gwendolin was asking politely what Rose's speciality was. Bob held a dripping spiky snail up for Eva's admiration. 'I suppose Eva's told you about me and Dan,' Rose said silkily.

'That's where I recognise you from.' Gwendolin snapped her fingers in satisfaction. 'The university party. You were the girl I bumped into when I was leaving. Sorry about that. I was in rather a hurry.' She glanced at Eva apologetically. She'd left in a huff that day.

'It was all rather strange, Dan getting Eva onto Bob's expedition,' Rose said. 'And I know Eva won't mind me saying this, but Dan was on a classic rebound when they got together.'

'Pardon?' Gwendolin's voice was suddenly icy.

Rose blinked twice but went on, 'Didn't she tell you? Oh Eva, I'm so sorry, I've let the cat out of the bag. I thought your mother knew you had stolen Dan from me.' She put her fingers delicately to her mouth as if shocked at her own words. Her blue eyes were round with innocence.

Bob found something of interest in a rock pool further away. Gwendolin stood rigid, staring at Rose. Eva was glad her mother's hat was on militarily straight. She looked every inch the successful professor. 'Is that what you think?' Gwendolin said pityingly.

Rose blinked again, suddenly confused. Gwendolin took a step forward, the crunch of tiny shells loud between them. Rose stepped back. 'From what I've seen, their relationship is one of strength and devotion, Rosie. Have I let the cat out of the bag? The truth can be painful.' This last was said softly to Rose.

Rose opened and shut her mouth. 'It's Rose, not Rosie,' she said lamely. 'I . . .'

Gwendolin lifted her head, 'You . . . ?'

Rose shook her head. She stepped back carefully again and then walked fast and then faster until she was practically running back up to the huts.

'A relationship of strength and devotion?' Eva said with amusement. At that moment she was utterly proud of her mother.

Gwendolin laughed. 'Did I over-egg it?'

'Let's just say I've never heard you endorse relationships quite so powerfully. Especially when you know that Dan and I are not officially in one; it's more complicated than that. But thank you for standing up for me.'

Then Gwendolin amazed her by putting her arms around her and hugging tightly. Eva stood within the circle of her mother's embrace, smelling her light flowery perfume, and then slowly she hugged her back. 'I do love you,' Gwendolin said, her voice suspiciously croaky. 'I just don't know how to show it sometimes.'

'You never show it,' Eva said honestly, 'but I don't care now. I'll know it's there. You vanquished Rose after all and that's not easy.'

They both watched the girl in the lemon dress, who was sitting now on a bench outside the huts, her long pale hair shining in the sunshine.

'You need to watch that one,' Gwendolin warned. 'I've met people like her before. She's capable of doing great harm. Make sure it's not to you.'

'I'll take care,' Eva promised. She wasn't bothered about Rose. It was so much more important that Gwendolin had opened up to her.

'And Eva?'

'Yes?'

'I am proud of you. I shouldn't have sent the letter, I can see that now. You are making your way just fine. I won't ask about the state of your relationship with Dan despite what Rose has let slip. Just promise me you won't get hurt?'

Eva nodded. 'I promise. Look, Bob's waving you over. Why don't you join him? I'll make iced tea and bring it down. Daisy's bound to want to join us.'

Daisy had already made iced tea and found a packet of shortbread biscuits from the supply bag. Eva helped her find glasses and plates. The divers were a messy lot and items were scattered about in no particular order, which was odd considering how meticulous they all were when it came to their scuba-diving gear.

'What's got Rose's goat?' Daisy asked. 'She nearly bit my head off for asking if she'd like a cup of tea with us. Stomped off back to camp. She's such a strange creature.'

'Don't worry about her,' Eva said. 'Let's go and make the most of the afternoon.'

She looked out of the hut window, always keen to soak in the view. And it was a stunning one, as usual: a glittering, coruscating sea under endless pastel skies, the turquoise patches where corals grew close under the water's surface and the darker, richer hues of valleys and trenches where who knew what fish lurked in the silent depths. The frigate birds soared high in the midday heat over the water, their forked tails trailing behind them. Beyond that, at the green fringes of the jungle cliffs, the vultures were circling and waiting.

Down at the edge of the sea, Bob and Gwendolin were wandering slowly. And then it clicked in Eva's mind, like a piece of jigsaw puzzle that had kicked about for ages in the box so long that it was familiar and ignored. But slotted into place, it made perfect sense, made the picture whole.

Eva managed to get Gwendolin to herself after the tea and biscuits by offering to show her the hidden bay beyond the rocky outcrop. It wasn't far away, but sufficient distance for privacy.

'Why didn't you tell me?' Eva said calmly.

'What are you talking about?' But Gwendolin lacked conviction. She knew exactly what Eva meant.

'You and Bob. How long's it been going on?'

'How did you find out?' Gwendolin asked. She stopped as they reached the hidden bay and looked at Eva.

'I saw you there on the beach. You looked like a couple, heads bent together. But I'm right, aren't I?' Eva kept walking onto the pure, smooth golden sand in the bay. Gwendolin had to follow. She sighed.

'Yes, you're right. Bob and I have been having an on-off affair for years. It's more than casual but less than committed. I can't really describe it properly myself.'

'Is that why you really came to Trinita?' Eva asked. 'Not because of me after all — so you could continue your affair?' There was a bitter taste in her mouth. She thought she had her mother all figured out and then in the blink of an eye the picture had changed.

'No, darling, you're wrong,' Gwendolin cried. 'I told you the truth. I came for you. Bob did ask me if I wanted to join him at the beginning of the summer and I'd played with the idea. But in the end, I came because I wanted to help you and to get through to you.'

'Get through to me? What do you mean?'

'I've felt for a long time that we've been living such separate lives in that London house. It's my fault — I've been so busy and as I said, I'm not the best mother role model. So, coming here was an attempt to clear the air and let you know that I'm on your side. Bob made it easy for me by inviting me here.

But I can see him back in London or wherever. I don't need to seek him out.'

'I believe you,' Eva said quietly. And she did. It made sense. 'I'm glad you came out here for me. And I don't disapprove of you and Bob being together. I'm glad you've got someone who makes you happy. Dad clearly didn't.'

Gwendolin dragged her toes into the sand, making little circles and sweeps. She avoided Eva's gaze. 'While we're being so honest with each other, I've another confession to make. Your father and I . . . we were cruel to each other. We couldn't live together without fighting, you know that. But you've always thought that Dad left me for Nancy. And I let you think it.'

'But it wasn't true,' Eva interrupted, the jigsaw pieces snapping together one after the other now. 'You and Bob were having an affair and Dad found out.'

Gwendolin nodded. Her toes dug in deep in the thick sand. 'I think I wanted him to find out. I wanted the marriage to be over with no way back. Your father left because of my affair. He didn't meet Nancy until quite some time later.'

'All this time, I've blamed him. And you let me!' Eva was appalled. She sat down heavily on the sand, regardless of the damp seeping into her shorts.

Gwendolin sat right down next to her. 'I was scared. This sounds silly but I thought you'd prefer him to me, that you'd go and live in New York permanently and I'd lose you. So I let you think he'd done that.'

Eva's headache, never far away, pounded on her temples with a vengeance. So many confused emotions. Yet out of it all, there was the knowledge that her mother loved her and had done these things out of love for her. She couldn't overlook that.

'I forgive you,' she whispered. She leaned her shoulder onto Gwendolin's and the two of them sat in the hidden bay, looking out at the gentle lapping waves.

11

Dan was working in a sunny courtyard at the back of the hospital in Verive. There was a queue of shabbily dressed people waiting patiently to see him and numerous small children were running about. In the centre of the courtyard there were a table and two chairs. A nun sat behind the table, on one of the chairs, writing in a notebook. Dan hunkered down in front of the table, so that he was better able to talk to an old woman so bent with age she was doubled over. A noise made him glance up and with a shock he saw Rose there in front of him, sighing happily at the sight of him. She skipped playfully to the top of the queue, nudging a skinny woman and her sickly baby out of line.

He masked his expression quickly and gave her a neutral smile. 'Rose, I wasn't expecting you here. Have you business in Verive? Is Bob here?'

That seemed to annoy her. 'Bob. Why would I be here with Bob? He's a silly old duffer. Ha, ha, just joking. No, I borrowed the jeep, although Anton was quite nasty about it.' She smoothed her features. 'Darling, I'm here to see you,' she went on breathily, leaning forward to give him a view of her breasts. 'It's a little surprise.'

'I'm busy.' Dan nodded to the woman she'd ousted and reached out for the child in her arms. Rose stepped sideways to avoid their touch. Her nose wrinkled up in disgust and he wondered why he'd ever thought her beautiful.

'I can see you're busy now, but you have to stop for lunch, don't you? My treat,' she said sweetly.

He was concentrating on putting a stethoscope to the baby's chest. It gave a rattling cough. Rose put her hand over her mouth as if to ward off germs. 'Dan?'

'Lunch then. But it'll have to be quick,' he said.

'Great, see you then.'

Dan was late. There were so many people who needed him. It was hard to have to tell them to wait while he had a short break for lunch. It didn't feel right, but he was exhausted as he'd worked so long. He caught sight of Rose before she saw him. She sat on a bench in the dusty town square waiting for him, her face getting gradually angrier and angrier. Finally she saw him, striding towards her, and put her sweetest face on.

'Darling, you must be so tired from healing all those people. Have a seat here. Let me feed you.'

'Thanks for the food. I didn't get time for breakfast this morning.' He helped himself to bread and grilled plantain and started eating.

Rose picked at a tomato and tore a tiny lump of bread from the loaf. 'I was hoping we could talk,' she said softly.

'About what?' He took a swig of the weak local beer she'd purchased, then flipped the lid off the other bottle and offered it to her.

Rose shook her head with a grimace. He'd forgotten how picky she was with food and drink. He should really offer to buy some other drink for her but he didn't have the energy.

'About what,' she mocked gently, then put her hand on his arm with pleasure as if admiring how nice her nails looked, buffed and polished against his skin. 'About us, Dan.'

His face hardened. He moved his arm away so her fingers fell to her lap. 'There is no 'us', Rose. When are you going to understand that?'

'You don't mean that. We've both done and said things we regret, but that was the past. We can move on into the future together.' She let her voice get a little tremulous with emotion.

'No. It's over. How could I ever trust you? First Sean, then James. How many others have there been?' Dan's voice was harsh. He put up his hand, blocking her when she made to answer. 'Actually I don't care what you might say to that. The fact is I fell out of love with you the day I found you and Sean together. It's just taken me a while to realise it.'

'But I love you,' she said desperately. 'I'll make it up to you, I promise. Just give me the opportunity to try.'

'I don't love you,' Dan said bluntly, rising up from the bench and staring at her hard. 'Get it into your head, Rose. Find someone else to play your games with.'

She jumped up too, incensed by him. 'You love *her*, do you? You're mistaken. She's not worth loving. She's using you, that's all.'

'I love Eva,' Dan said, a soft quality to his tone that he couldn't hide. 'I haven't told her yet but yes, I do. I'm sorry Rose, but it would never have worked with us. We're too different.' He walked away back towards the hospital and the courtyard of patients.

Rose clenched her fists and shouted after him, 'You'll be sorry, Dan Adams. You won't get away with treating me like this. I'm warning you!'

But Dan kept on walking evenly, ignoring her. Behind him there was a shriek of fury. He heard her get into the jeep and slam the door hard. She clearly wasn't going to give him a lift back to camp. The jeep suddenly careered past him and screeched to a halt. Rose wound the window down and shouted out of it. She was so angry that a spray of spittle landed on the glass.

'If I can't have you, then Eva Martinez won't have you either. I'll think of something!' The jeep jumped away in a cloud of diesel and sand, leaving him there aghast. Her threat hung in the dusty air. She was angry with him, he reasoned. It was an empty gesture, unkind but not dangerous.

* * *

Dan couldn't concentrate in the afternoon. He sounded chests, listened to lungs, gave injections and prescribed creams and ointments, but his mind was elsewhere. Eventually he passed the last remaining patients over to the care of Sister Naomi and decided he had to get back to camp. He needed to tell Eva what he'd revealed to Rose. He was in love with her. Why hadn't he admitted it before now? He had told himself he couldn't bear to be hurt again. But his love for Eva had overpowered him. Without her, life had no meaning. And unless he told her how he felt, soon they would go their separate ways at the end of the expedition.

She had been quiet since they returned from visiting Angelica. He hadn't pressed her to find out what was wrong, hoping she trusted him enough to explain. But she hadn't. He needed to be in Verive to run his clinic and her mother was arriving at the camp in any case. Perhaps that was the diversion Eva needed. He tidied up his medical bag and said goodbye to the hospital staff.

Waiting for the local bus, he was glad Rose hadn't offered him a lift. They needed space now that the air was cleared between them. She would come round to it in time and see he was right. They were no good together. He had thought he was in love with her but his feelings for Eva were a thousand times stronger than what he'd ever felt for Rose. He'd been taken in by Rose's beauty and her veneer of gentle femininity. But scratch beneath the surface and another Rose emerged. One he didn't like at all.

The camp was quiet when he got back. It was late and the fire was lit. Daisy and Sam sat by it, chatting. Bob and Gwendolin were examining boxes of specimens. He briefly introduced himself to Eva's mother, who was polite without warmth. He scanned the camp for Eva.

'Tent,' Daisy called, knowing him too well.

He went in to find her sitting on her low bed.

She brightened visibly when she saw him and Dan's heart quickened. He longed to run his fingers through her thick, dark curly hair and lift her face to his for a kiss that lasted forever. But first, he had to tell her that he'd fallen in love with her. He only hoped she felt the same way. She was quick to tell him that it was it was just a casual attraction between the two of them, that night in the jeep coming home from the beach. But things were different now. It was as if he saw the world afresh through new eyes. He longed for her. But not simply physically. He wanted a joining of souls. He wanted to know her innermost feelings. He wanted them to be as one. Was all this written on his face? Eva smiled tentatively. He was about to tell her but she spoke first.

'Did you meet my mother?'

It wasn't what he expected her to say. A little taken aback, he nodded.

'What did she say?' Eva asked curiously. She picked a thread from her shorts.

'She was somewhat frosty,' Dan said with a grin. 'Asked me if I was treating you well. Used the word 'sponsor' as if it were a dirty rag.'

Eva smiled weakly and rubbed her face. 'You told me recently that we didn't know each other very well. That you were sure there were things about me you didn't know. And it's true.'

Dan was heartened. This was what he wanted, to get to know her better. 'What is it?' he asked gently.

'My mother, Gwendolin. She wrote to Bob about me. About how I might not be up to the job. That was why Bob called me into his tent. He wanted to discuss the letter and know whether he could trust me to do my work.'

'What!' Dan was incredulous. 'Why would your own mother stab you in the back like that?'

'No, no, it's not like that,' Eva sighed. 'It's difficult to explain. She had my best interests at heart. Believe it or not, I feel closer to her now than I've ever done. But she told me something about her and my father that I hadn't known. It changes everything.'

If only he could smooth the crease of

anxiety away from her brow. It would be a tender gesture, for it meant love and commitment and caring. All of these were true for him. But he had yet to confess them. And what about Eva? Would she return his feelings? 'Is it serious?' he asked her.

'I haven't spoken to my father since before the summer,' Eva said. 'We had a huge argument and at the end of it I flung at him that he had abandoned my mother for his affair with Nancy. He in turn shouted that I'd always preferred my mother to him. It was all a bit child-ish, looking back at it.'

'Can't you make up?'

'I don't know. It turns out I completely misjudged him. It was my mother having the affair which broke up the marriage. What on earth should I say to him?'

Dan took her hand. She didn't pull away. 'Say sorry,' he said simply, 'Ask if you can forgive each other. He's your father. He's not going to walk away from you.'

'He's a strong character,' Eva replied doubtfully.

'So are you,' Dan said. 'You can do this. Go to him once the expedition's finished. Tell him what you need to. You're the strongest woman I know.'

Eva crinkled her lovely grey eyes and smiled. 'Thank you,' she said.

He leaned in towards her. 'Eva . . . ' But he didn't need to speak because she was drawing him closely to her as if her life depended on it. The tent was an oasis, the material sheltering them from the dark evening and the people in the camp beyond. He broke from her momentarily to zip the entrance, then returned to her embrace.

She pulled him down to lie with her on the camp bed. It was narrow for two and she giggled as he tried to find space before kissing him with such warmth and passion he wanted to cry out. 'I love you,' he whispered. 'I came to tell you that. It took me a while to realise it but it's true.'

'And I love you too,' Eva said,

trembling with her emotion. 'I can't bear to be apart from you.'

With a stifled groan, he kissed her again from the corner of her lips in a burning trail down her neck to the soft hollows below. 'Make love to me,' she whispered desperately, kissing him in return and turning to pull the covers up over them both.

It was sweet and tender and more than he'd imagined it would be, taking them both to an exquisite crescendo of love and desire and leaving them hungry for more. But Dan knew they had the rest of their lives to learn about each other. Their privacy in the tent could be shattered at any moment. They dressed and sat, not needing to talk, but each revelling in what had happened and the joy of finding out that they both felt the same way.

Eva held his hand and he squeezed her fingers gently. If only they were alone together somewhere quite private. Would she like his house in the London suburbs? Or would she want to live in

America? With a jolt, Dan realised he wanted to marry Eva and live with her immediately. He couldn't bear the thought of being without her. It felt right. It was perfect and he knew without a doubt that he'd love her forever.

There was a loud interruption as the canvas was brushed aside and Sam's head appeared, looking worried. 'Dan, you must come. Immediately.'

'What is it, Sam? What's happened?' He found he was still clutching Eva's hand. It felt warm and comforting and yet shot through with a tingling awareness. Her fingers curled round his as Sam spoke urgently.

'It's Rose. She's vanished.'

12

They formed a search party. It was made up of Dan, Sam, Bob, Anton and two others from Rose's team. Daisy was to stay behind in case Rose showed up back at camp. Gwendolin refused to go, saying she was going to sit with Eva, who was feeling unwell again. The men readied themselves swiftly, taking water bottles and some food supplies.

'Dan, there's something you should see,' Sam said, as Dan was about to call the group together and start the search. He handed over a folded piece of paper, his usually good-natured face stiff with unease.

Dan opened the paper and scanned.

Darling Dan
By the time you are reading this, I shall be long gone from here. I can't bear a life without you. I love you so

*much and I know you love me too
even if you won't admit it. We are
meant to be together. If you love me
then show it and find me darling.*
  Yours forever
  Rose

Dan's lips tightened grimly. He gave
it back to Sam without a word. Blast
Rose. She was ill. That was the only
explanation. He had told her several
times now that he wasn't interested in
her. He wasn't in love with her
anymore. But she couldn't accept it.
She was unbalanced in her mind. She
needed help. And he had a duty to her
to get that help. He had to find Rose
and persuade her to leave Trinita for
London. If he had to pay her ticket
himself then that was what he would
do.

'Let's go,' he said to Sam.

But Sam caught his arm. 'Don't go.
Let the rest of us find her. There's
something not right about this.'

Dan shook his head. 'She's my

responsibility, Sam. I have to find her.' The two men exchanged a look. Sam gave a brief nod. Dan knew he wasn't happy with his decision but also that he had Sam at his back in the search and that gave him a measure of comfort.

The others were ready to go. Bob had taken charge. Head torches had been distributed as the light was fading fast. 'Once we're in the jungle, we'll split up and radiate out. That's the best way to cover the widest range. Rose has had at least an hour's gain on us. She could be anywhere. I am concerned at her state of mind.' He paused and passed round the paper Rose had written. 'I hope we're in time.'

What was Bob implying? Dan took the paper and re-read it. Of course. What a fool he was. What Rose had written could be a suicide note. Was she deranged enough to take her own life? There was no way of knowing. On first reading, he'd interpreted her words as a challenge to him. If he cared for her, he'd find her. And once he did, he would never be free of her because it would confirm in her mind that he did indeed love her. It was a no-win situation. For he could hardly leave her to wander the forest. Now, he wasn't sure what he would find: Rose alive and triumphant in the face of evidence he loved her, or her lifeless body. These grim thoughts accompanied him as the search party fanned out. He'd barely had a moment to speak to Gwendolin as they passed.

'Look after Eva for me. Tell her we'll talk more when I return.'

Gwendolin had shot him an icy glare. 'My daughter is feverish. If you have any kind of *real* feelings for her, you'd be at her side now, instead of gallivanting off after your ex-lover.' She wanted him to make a choice. But Dan couldn't, now that Bob had hinted that Rose was in danger of dying at her own hand. Eva would understand even if her mother didn't. He didn't have time to explain.

'Just tell her,' he said. He followed

the rest of them by the trail and the bruised leaves and frayed branches where the machetes had hacked. He saw the back of a bush shirt as someone ahead of him, possibly Sam judging by his height, vanished to the west. Faint bobbing lights were visible from the head torches. They had separated almost immediately, which made sense for searching but was disheartening for morale. Dan was alone, enclosed by the sweating vegetation. Humidity was high tonight, with one tropical downpour early on and another promised by the circle of smoky sky barely visible above him amongst the canopy foliage.

He tried to think as Rose might do. Where would she go to wait for him? He didn't think about the other possibility, and blanked it out. If she wanted to kill herself then she could be anywhere. No, he had to imagine that she wanted to surprise him. She would want a dramatic backdrop for their reunion, as she would see it. Then it came to him. Lunara Gorge. About half an hour's walk from camp, beyond the caves that he and Eva had explored, was a mile-long gash in the earth. A chasm which disappeared hundreds of metres to a narrow bottom of rotting leaf litter and a thin stream.

He tried to think whether Rose would know about it. Then he remembered. The night they had sat about the camp fire, Bob had brought up the subject of the Lunara Gorge. He warned them to be careful when out surveying. The lip of the Gorge was not obvious due to ferns and vines and he didn't want anyone slipping over the edge. Hadn't Rose then queried him about the gorge's whereabouts? Dan couldn't remember but it was worth a shot. There wasn't a more dramatic backdrop of scenery around. He decided to make for the Gorge and prayed he'd find her there.

It was a beautiful place to be under ordinary circumstances. The threat of rain held off and Dan walked through a wilderness of colourful flowers, luminous in the dark, and gaudy night moths in glades where massive tree trunks had fallen. From these sentinels, ferns and pitcher plants grew up, a reminder that life finds a way even in death. Leaf-cutter ants paraded along the bark, waving their bright green cuts above their heads. An olive dove flew up in front of him, cooing softly. He heard the squabble of macaws, unseen except where the branches shook high up. There was the spoor of a large cat in the damp mud of the trail. A jaguar had passed this way. Dan wasn't worried. Whatever it was didn't continue in the direction he was going. Besides, like most forest animals, it would shy away from him unless he confronted it. Which he wasn't likely to do.

He stopped to wipe the sweat from his brow. It wasn't far now. He listened for the others. Nothing. He wondered where they were. Bob had mentioned the caves, so it seemed probable he'd headed that way. Sam was going to alert the divers, then circle round and re-join the jungle. Anton and his crew had huddled for a few minutes before spreading out. Whatever their plan was, they hadn't chosen to share it. He guessed at least two of them had gone south, which covered areas he, Bob and Sam wouldn't get to. It made sense.

He almost walked over the edge before he realised. Lunara Gorge. He'd arrived. He stopped abruptly, heart lurching and his foot half over empty space. With great care he stepped back onto solid ground. The edge was slippery, with soft mud and leaf mulch between the ferns' roots. A troop of howler monkeys bellowed in the tree-tops and the trees swayed as they leapt along. Something or someone had disturbed them.

There was a pink thing caught on a twig. His torch light picked it out. He went to it, very aware of the edge of the chasm on his left. It was a scrap of material. Rose had been wearing a pink cotton dress when she turned up in

Verive. It had to be from her.

He pulled it free and tucked it into his trouser pocket. Where was she? He didn't want to think about the bottom of the gorge. He made a wide detour round a huge buttress root and came to a halt. Rose stood there. She was standing on an outcrop of granite that teetered out over the wide space of the chasm. Its surface was strangely devoid of vegetation, though the rock faces going down were bearded with vines and tangled roots.

'Hello, Dan.' She was calm and smiling. Her smile made the tiny hairs on the back of his neck stand up.

'Rose, I'm glad I found you. It's not safe here. You need to come over to me.'

'It's safe enough. I knew you'd come. You couldn't resist me. I told her that.'

'Told who?'

'You know who,' Rose said, winding a strand of her blonde hair round a finger and cocking her head flirtatiously. 'It's a guessing game. You're good at games, Dan. We've played a few together, haven't we?'

Eva. That was who she meant. But Dan didn't want to say Eva's name in case it sent Rose into a rage. The outcrop was narrow and the rock damp. He had to get her off there and onto firm ground.

'Okay. Why don't you come over here and we'll talk?' Dan beckoned her, backing away from the gorge as he spoke, hoping she'd follow.

'I don't think so. Not yet. I tore my dress,' she said sadly, showing him the rip in the hem.

'It doesn't matter, I'll buy you a new dress,' Dan said, trying not to let the desperation show in his voice. How long was it going to take to talk her down? The longer she stood there, the more chance of a slip. And if she went down, there was little chance of a good outcome.

'Darling, would you? That's so good of you. It makes me think that you love me just a little bit. Do you, Dan? Do you love me? If you say you do, then I'll take a step towards you.' She made a moue of her lips and blew him a kiss. Her eyes were such an intense shade of blue, like a morpho butterfly sheen. And in them he saw madness.

'You need help, Rose,' he said gently. 'I'm going to get you to safety and call your father to come and get you.'

'That's so typical of you,' she spat at him, her face ugly with sudden anger. 'Dan Adams, always the gentleman, doing the right thing. That's why I slept with Sean. I wanted to wake you up. I wanted to see you angry, fighting Sean over me. But you didn't, did you? You walked away instead. So controlled. So . . . so *righteous*! I hate you, I hate you.' She shook with her venom and Dan lunged forward to grab her as she wobbled sideways.

As he reached for her, Rose's eyes widened in satisfaction. At the last moment she stepped aside. Dan fell over the edge of the outcrop. Into nothing.

13

Eva was dreaming. In her dreams she was running through the undergrowth but getting slower and slower. The vines tugged at her legs and the ground was soaked in treacle. She sank deep into it, and pulling each leg out tired her. She was trying to reach someone but she didn't know who. Only that she had to get to them. It was a matter of life and death. She tossed and turned in her bed, moaning, fighting her cotton sheet as it wound around her. She was damp with sweat, which chilled on her skin. Shivering, she ran on, disorientated. Above her a shrieking witch swooped. She ducked, looked up, and saw Rose's distorted face hovering over her. Spit from her mouth landed like hot coals on Eva's cheek. Rose was screeching words. A man's name. Over and over. Dan, Dan, Dan. Where was Dan?

Eva sat bolt upright, crying out his name. 'Dan!'

It brought Gwendolin running to her. She mopped Eva's streaming forehead with a cool cloth. 'It's all right. They're looking for him now. You can't do anything. You must lie down and rest.'

'What do you mean? Where is he?' Eva pushed at her mother frantically. She wasn't making sense. She had to get up and out of bed. She had to be strong. What was going on? She needed Dan. Then it came back to her. Rose was missing. Dan and Bob with the others had gone searching for her. So why were they now looking for Dan?

Eva tried to lift her legs out of bed. They were so heavy and when she moved them, stabs of pain went right into her thigh muscles. Her head spun dizzily. She was faint.

'No, no. You stay right there,' Gwendolin ordered, pushing her back gently onto the pillow. 'You'll do no one any favours by trying to help.'

'What's wrong with me?' Eva whispered.

Gwendolin fussed with the bed sheet, attempting to untangle it. 'You've got a fever of some kind. Until we get Dan to treat you, all I can do is give you plenty of fluids and make sure you rest.'

'Dan?' Eva asked again.

Gwendolin shook her head helplessly. There was a noise of commotion outside: a woman's high-pitched cry, and then Bob's deep bellowing commands.

'Wait here,' Gwendolin warned.

Eva couldn't move if she tried. She lay back, wondering what was going on. Her head swirled unpleasantly. She'd contracted a jungle virus, that was certain. Now, more than ever, she wanted Dan. She needed his cool competence and reassuring hands to make her better. More than that, she had to have him near for the sake of her soul. He made her complete. She was glad she'd told him when she had a chance. *I love you, Dan.* She cried it out in her mind. Could he feel it, wherever he was right now? Feel the intensity of her love for him, carried on the wind?

Then Gwendolin was back. 'It's Rose,' she said. 'She found her way back. She's an absolute mess. I don't know what kind of trauma she's been through, and she's not making a lot of sense.'

'And Dan?' Eva could hardly bring herself to ask. Her whole body trembled as she waited for her mother to answer.

'No, there's no sign of him.'

'Did Rose see him out there?' Eva wiped her lips with the back of her hand. They were dry and cracked and painful.

'It's hard to tell what she's seen. She's muttering all sorts. But she didn't mention him.'

'Go and ask!' Eva snapped.

Gwendolin looked like she'd reprimand her but went after a slight pause. Perhaps she'd registered the desperation that Eva felt. It was as if her body was encased in cement and she couldn't move, but her mind was fighting to be free. The fog in her head came and went at short intervals.

The rasp of the tent entrance hurt her ears as Gwendolin reappeared. 'Darling, you mustn't upset yourself. I'm sure it won't help you recover.'

'Just tell me. Please. Where is he?'

Her mother sat on the end of the camp bed. It made Eva's body cry out in pain. It reminded her of having the flu a few years ago when she was at high school. Gwendolin had hired a day nurse for her. There was no slot in her busy schedule to care for her ill daughter. Besides, it wasn't in her nature to tend to the sick. So she ought to be grateful now that Gwendolin was here beside her. Instead she felt only irritation that she wasn't able to tell her about Dan.

'Rose claims she didn't see him. Her story is that she wrote her note while planning to kill herself. She went off into the jungle and wandered about until she realised she wanted to live. Apparently her love for Dan kept her going, along with the knowledge that his love for her was even greater.'

'And now? What's she doing?' Eva's lip was bleeding where she'd pressed her teeth against it.

Gwendolin lifted her palms to indicate her puzzlement. 'She's alternating between ranting about you and weeping about her lost love. To be honest, we all think she's in need of some serious medical attention. Bob's organising for her to be sent to the hospital in Verive until he can contact her next of kin. In the meantime she's under a kind of guard in her tent — Anton's standing outside in case she makes another run for it.'

Eva knew she should feel sorry for Rose. The jungle had proved too much for her. Dan was right, she was too delicate to deal with the raw power of its nature. But she wished Rose had never come here. She couldn't prove it but her instinct cried out that Rose had something to do with Dan's disappearance.

'You get a bit of sleep,' Gwendolin said. 'I'm going to make sure Bob's not overdoing it. He's very stressed out with how his expedition's turned out.'

Alone in the tent, Eva lay back and stared at the ceiling. A bright green beetle like a live emerald was tracking along the material. When it reached the apex, it stopped. Where was Dan? The fog in her mind cleared a little. What was the most dangerous place within reasonable walking distance of the camp? She thought of the caves. She'd almost drowned in there — would have, if Dan hadn't released her leg from the rocks. It was possible he'd gone there looking for Rose. An image of him trapped and dead under the rushing cave stream made her cry out. The beetle was moving again. It walked the straight line of the top of the tent between the 'v' of the sides, as if it was in a beetle-sized crevasse. And then it clicked. Eva knew where Dan was. The greatest crevasse she'd ever seen. Lunara Gorge.

She fell out of bed and half-crawled to the flap. It took all her strength to unzip it. The fog had descended once more, thick and confusing and pounding on her skull. Still, she threw her body outside, hitting the hard ground. She had to tell someone. They had to go now. If Dan really was near the gorge then he was in serious trouble. She wouldn't even imagine a worse scenario. No one could survive a fall into the gorge.

But there was no one around. They were all out looking for Dan, but in the wrong place. Surely if they'd got to Lunara they would have found him by now. Sick though she was, Eva knew she had to get there and find him. She had to go fast before Gwendolin stopped her. She wasn't thinking clearly. Acting on instinct, she stumbled through the jungle, at first walking, and then when it became too difficult, crawling in the undergrowth but never,

never giving up.

Sam found her at the edge of the gorge, struggling to get to her feet and to get onto the lip of the chasm. He lifted her up and she collapsed into his arms. 'Dan's down there. Help him, Sam. Help him,' she pleaded, then blacked out. Two more men from Rose's team arrived and Sam gave her over to them with orders to take her back to camp. Then he turned back to the gorge.

When she came round, Eva was back in her bed. At first she couldn't work out where she was and what had happened. It was dark outside. She could see the night air. Someone had carelessly left the zip half open and the mosquitoes were inside. She'd been bitten several times. She could feel the itchy lumps on her face, her arms, even one finger. How many hours had passed? She moved her head to the side and her chest tightened in shock. Rose sat there on the edge of Dan's bed, watching her. Her blonde hair was lank and straggly. Her blue eyes were shiny and strangely blank. Her smile gave Eva the creeps.

'You're awake. Finally. I've been waiting for ages.' Her voice was sing-song and she moved her head side to side like a praying mantis.

'Where's Anton?' Eva managed out of a parched throat. Her words were raspy, unclear.

Rose leaned towards her to catch what she'd said and Eva shrank back involuntarily. There was an aura to Rose. A sour lingering note around her, inchoate and repulsive.

'Anton's rather stupid,' Rose laughed. 'He's easily diverted. I threw stones from under the back of my tent until he went off to see what was going on. Then I slipped out over here. Don't worry, no one saw me. I can stay as long as you like.'

As if Eva wanted her there at all. There was a chumminess in her statement that sat uneasily with what was in her eyes. 'What do you want with me?' Eva asked, trying to put strength into her voice and failing miserably. She coughed. Her throat was agony. She needed water.

Rose lifted the water canister from the ground next to the bed, where Gwendolin had left it. She let it hover in her hand near Eva, then deliberately set it down out of reach. 'Are you the gambling sort?' she asked, conversationally.

Eva simply stared. Her head was stuffed with cotton wool, her T-shirt chilled with cold sweat from the waves of fever. She was thirsty and her limbs ached. Where were Sam and Dan? Had she managed to save him? Why didn't Anton return and discover Rose was missing from her tent? What was Rose going to do? She looked capable of anything, as if all ordinary boundaries of behaviour had vaporized.

'Come on,' Rose snapped impatiently. 'Wake up, Eva. Let's bet on Dan. When he comes back . . . '

'*Is* he coming back?' Eva interrupted,

using up too much of her energy doing so. 'What did you do to him?'

'I love Dan and he loves me. He'll be back.' Rose shook her head as if a fly bothered her. She pressed the heel of her hand to her eye socket. Then more brightly, looked at Eva. Her teeth were ever so white. Eva noticed how sharp, how pointed her canines looked. A tiny but vicious predator came to mind.

'Anyway.' Rose tossed her hair, seemingly oblivious to its greasy rat-tails. 'The question is, will he come back to me or to you? What do you wager?'

Anton pushed his way into the tent. It was crowded. 'There you are, Rose. Please come back with me to your tent. Eva needs peace.' He brooked no argument.

Rose grabbed at Eva's arm. Her nails bit into her flesh. 'Me or you?' she shouted as Anton politely but firmly steered her away. 'Remember that, Eva Martinez. He'll be too busy loving me to bother with you. You'll wait in vain.'

* ★ ★

Dan assessed the damage. He must've fallen unconscious for a few minutes. Or longer. It was hard to say. He was lying on a narrow ledge, maybe fifty or so metres below the lip of the gorge. His shirt was snagged on thorny curved vines. They had saved him from falling to the bottom. Such a fragile link between him and life. But he was caught in them as surely as a fly in a web. The stone under him was slimy and brittle. Any movement sent flakes scattering down into the void. His medical training made him start at his head and work mentally down his body for injury.

He was suffering from concussion. He felt the back of his skull gingerly. There was a painful lump the size of a goose egg. His head ached and a wave of nausea washed over him. His vision was okay but when he tried to focus on the other side of the gorge there was a faint blurriness to it. It wasn't good. He needed hospital treatment. If he blacked out again . . .

Calmly, he continued with his medical assessment. His upper body didn't appear to be in any pain. But the same couldn't be said for his legs. They had borne the weight of his fall. He'd toppled head over heels and landed on his right leg hard. He knew immediately it was broken. He was lying on it. He tried to see it from his awkward position pinned to the thorny twigs. His lower leg was an odd shape. There was a white object protruding from a gash. It was his bone.

Dan looked up. Above him was a fringe of delicate ferns. Beyond that, the forest and a glimpse of dark but moonlit sky. Somehow he had to climb back up and out of the gorge. Where was Rose? Was she still out there, sitting on the forest floor? He called for her as loudly as he could manage. The birds sang back at him. Rose had tried to kill him. It was ludicrous, impossible, insane. But it had happened. Dan shut up. It was best she didn't find out that she hadn't succeeded. Might she try again? In his weakened, helpless state he was no match for her, tiny though she was.

The question was, could he put any weight on his right leg? It might mean the difference in surviving or not. He couldn't count on the others finding him here. He guessed that from the top, they wouldn't see him. The ferns hid him. If he fainted, then there'd be no noise to alert them. He needed to conserve his energy until he heard someone. Then he could only pray it was Bob or Sam and not Rose. It was a gamble. But he had no alternative.

He took a deep breath and attempted to get upright. His leg was agony. The thorns held him as tightly as a lover. He came round, realising he'd lost minutes. It was no good. His leg was not going to bear the rest of him. If he lost consciousness while climbing he would die. He hung there, gathering what little strength he had. He would not give in to despair. It wasn't in his nature. He had to get back to Eva. This one thought kept him going. It was his focus, his burning light. But how?

The hours stretched. Eventually the slice of sky he could see segued into purple and navy. A bracelet of stars arrived. A flurry of bats flew over the gorge, hunting. A giant moth with two white eye rings on its wings fluttered past his head. It was the largest one he'd ever seen, easily the size of a sparrow. He wondered if he'd hallucinated it.

Then he heard it. Someone was up there. More than one person. He could hear them clearly, talking to each other. He couldn't make out the words. But there were people. He had to alert them. And quickly, before they left him. Dan struggled to move. The thorns held on. In fact, he was winding himself in further to them each time he rolled. A piece of ledge, the same size as the moth, broke off under his foot and he listened as it hit the side of the gorge and went into the void. He shouted up. But his voice was weak and thin. Then he remembered. In his shirt pocket he had matches. He'd lit the fire in the morning for breakfast, then absent-mindedly slid the remaining matches into the pocket instead of the box. If he could reach them, would anyone see the light?

Very carefully he reached for the pocket. His elbow was caught on the bush but he managed to get his fingers under the material. His fingertips touched the wooden strips. He felt three. He drew one out, curling it into his palm, and brought it back. If he could just strike it alight. He tried to get it to the rock face to use as a hard surface. The match slipped from his grasp. Dan cursed. He was running out of time. The people were up there, but for how long? He repeated his actions, forcing himself to be slow and deliberate. If he lost the last two matches he'd be out of options. The second match broke on the rock, the tiny sulphur head dropping uselessly away. All his hopes pinned on a final flimsy splinter of wood. The third match struck. A wisp of acrid smoke drifted to him. Then a flame. Yes. He'd done it.

One tiny match flame was hardly going to be noticed. Dan knew what he had to do. There was a large tuft of cream-coloured grass above him. He'd touched it. Noted it was almost dry. Now, he reached as far as he could in his prison and tipped the flame to the long leaves. If he'd prayed for fire, he was disappointed. The grass was too damp. With a long groan he sagged back. It was useless. He'd failed. The people would move on. Without medical attention he wouldn't last another day.

He smelt smoke. There was a coil of it rising up from the grass. Of course. It wasn't dry enough to go up in flame like tinder. But the damp made it fug. It was more effective. It wafted up in a hopeful column. There was an exclamation from high above. Shouts to and fro.

A long call down in query. Dan summoned up all his remaining strength and shouted back up the endless slope.

★ ★ ★

They brought him back to camp. Eva managed to get out of bed and Sam helped her over to where Dan was lying. He was conscious and breathed her name as she bent over him.

'You're safe,' she said, weeping, 'You're safe now, my love. Bob's phoning for medical help.'

'It was you,' Dan whispered. 'You found me. I heard you up there at the top of the gorge. You saved me.'

Eva collapsed beside him on the makeshift blanket, her fever overcoming her. Dan, too, lay still as his consciousness faded.

14

Jason and Nancy Martinez lived in a brownstone on a moderately busy street in a smart area of New York City. The entrance was an arched covered walkway manned by the same doorman Eva had grown up knowing. Marty Kozlowski gave his familiar salute when he saw her. He wore his uniform with military bearing and took his job seriously.

'Good afternoon, Miss Martinez. Good to see you home.'

'Hey, Marty. Thanks. Is my father in?'

'I saw him go out this morning, I'm guessing to work. But Mrs Martinez's there. Can I get you a hand with your luggage?'

Eva shook her head. 'I'll manage, thanks.'

She only had the small amount of gear she'd taken to Trinita with her. The bags were smeared with tropical dirt and there was a rip in her kitbag. Her departure from the island was a blur. She'd collapsed with fever after they'd brought Dan into the camp as fear and relief had mingled in her. Worried, Gwendolin and Bob had taken both her and Dan to the hospital in Verive despite the late hour, not daring to wait for the medical help promised from the big hospital so far south in Galanga. They'd had a treacherous journey in the dark. There she'd ended up in a small ward next door to Dan, who in turn lay in a bed next to James. The nuns had treated her well, reduced the fever and got some fluids into her. Within days, she was told she could leave. Gwendolin wanted her to go straight home to London. But Eva had insisted on staying until there was news of Dan's recovery. She was given the use of the same small house in the hospital grounds. Gwendolin was using it too.

'This is silly, darling. You should be

somewhere civilized to recuperate. I can buy you a ticket to London today. You could be home in a few hours.'

'I'm not going while Dan's lying here in an awful condition,' Eva told her for what seemed like the hundredth time.

'You don't know anything about this man, really,' Gwendolin argued. 'Maybe when he went missing after Rose, he wanted to disappear. People do that, you know. There's something shady in their past so they vanish, get a new identity and pop up somewhere else to start afresh.'

'That's ridiculous,' Eva said sharply. 'Dan wouldn't do that. And he didn't go into that gorge of his own volition, I'm sure of that.' She paced the small room in agitation.

Then Bob came in to tell them the latest update. 'They're air-lifting Dan to the States. Apparently the break in his leg is more complicated than they can deal with here. I'm sure it's nothing to be worried about, probably just being cautious, and rightly so in my opinion.'

That was when Eva knew she had to go to her father's house to recuperate. Back to New York. At least that way she'd be on the same continent as Dan. Gwendolin was very upset with her.

'You're going to New York? Why not back home to London? I'll be there.'

Eva gave her mother a quick squeeze hug. 'You know you hate being around sick people, admit it. I'll be no use to you in the house. I'll be sleeping and eating. It'll be a bore.'

'But going to your father — he's no better a nurse than me. London will be . . . '

'Better than New York?' Eva finished gently with amusement. 'No, both cities are crazy busy, just the way I like it. I'll be fine with Dad. Besides, we both know it'll be Nancy who looks after me.'

Gwendolin couldn't argue with that, but she continued to be hurt and upset by Eva's decision. She showed it by being cool and polite. Eva let her do it.

She'd come round eventually. Besides, although she wouldn't tell her mother, she still had it in mind to find a job in London by the autumn. First, she had to get rid of the post-viral fatigue which had settled on her like mist.

Nancy opened the door on Eva's second ring of the bell. She looked taken aback when she saw Eva but recovered quickly. 'Honey, how lovely to see you. We weren't expecting you.' Her warm, brash New Yorker accent hit Eva with all the familiarity of home.

'I didn't call ahead,' she explained. 'I thought I'd just come straight here.'

Nancy led the way into the large living room. She hadn't changed much over the years. Still the all-American cheerleader with her natural bright blonde hair swept up in a casual ponytail and her clear skin and slim body. She was in her late thirties now but looked ten years younger.

'How's Dad?' Eva asked. She dropped her bags at her feet. It was good to be home. She kicked off her shoes and sat back in one of the antique winged chairs.

Nancy sat too, perched on the edge of her chair. Her jogging pants and white sneakers looked out of place amongst the beautiful finery of the room. She must've been about to go out on her daily jog when Eva arrived. Now she looked nervous.

'Did you two make up yet?'

'No, I haven't spoken to him since I left here in the spring.'

'Well, he's your father so don't expect any apologies,' Nancy said, twisting her wedding ring on her finger.

Eva didn't. Her father was too like her: stubborn to the point of bull-headedness. Saying sorry was so difficult for both of them. Poor Nancy. Ever the peace-keeper. 'You're good for him,' she said, meaning it.

Nancy flushed prettily. 'I love him. But it's nice to hear you say that.'

'I didn't really appreciate you when I was growing up,' Eva went on. Some-how it was important that Nancy understood. 'I was a bit of a brat, wasn't I?'

Nancy laughed. 'You weren't easy. Kept telling me you had a mother already and didn't need a second one. Stroppy was your middle name.'

'Sorry.'

'Don't be. It was natural kid stuff. I love you anyway, whether you want me to or not.' Nancy patted Eva's head as if she was still a kid, half-joking.

'So what mood's he in then these days?' Eva asked, changing the subject. She'd cry otherwise. 'Has he talked about me?'

'Yeah, sure he talks about you. Speculates where you are, what you're doing, what you *should* be doing. You know your father, he always likes to be right.'

That was certain. He liked to be in control. He found it difficult when Eva made her own decisions and choices, even as she turned into an adult. The tiredness kicked in. She yawned. She'd been up at the crack of dawn to travel from Trinita to JFK airport. 'Is it okay if I crash for a bit?'

'Go on up,' Nancy said. 'Your room's the way you left it but there's fresh linen on the bed. I'll bring you up an iced tea.'

Jason Martinez arrived home later that day. Eva was lounging in the front room, flicking idly through one of Nancy's enormous pile of gossip magazines, too tired to put her sandals on and step outside into her favourite city. Tomorrow, she promised herself. Tomorrow she'd go. She'd find Dan and go to him. She didn't know which hospital he'd been airlifted to. But first she had to confront her father and she knew that Dan would understand. What was it he'd said, that day when he found her in her tent? *You're the strongest woman I know*. He believed in her. He believed in her more than anyone else she knew. One of the many, myriad reasons she loved him. Oh, to go to him right now. To run the city streets until she reached the hospital. To burst into his ward and wrap her arms around him, kiss him and *tell* him that again. She had first to find out which hospital he was in. But wherever he was, he was safe and so she had to bite back the urge to see him right then. First, she had to speak to her father.

He flung open the door and stood in the doorway, swinging his briefcase. His shirt was damp with perspiration and his tie was low where he'd pulled it free from his throat. New York was hot with summer.

'You didn't call.' No smile, no welcome hug for his daughter. His grey eyes, so uncannily like her own, bored into her.

Eva noticed the white in his dark curly hair, tinging his temples. There were crow lines radiating out from the corners of his eyes. Surely they were deeper than when she'd last seen him. Then the words. Did he mean she hadn't called ahead, like Nancy had commented? Or did he mean she hadn't called to apologise after their blazing row?

'Well, I'm here now.' Equally bullish and uncompromising. Her father brought out the worst in her. Her jaw tightened, ready for a fight, despite her weariness.

He laughed harshly. 'Staying? I bet not. Licking your wounds after some spat, I'll guess. Heaven forbid you'd come to settle.' He read her too easily.

'Let's not argue over this again,' Eva said, irritated, 'or I'll be sorry I did come to you instead of Mum's.'

'Mum? She lets you call her that now?' he mocked, knowing full well what the answer was. He stopped, pushed his briefcase aside with one expensively leather-shod shoe and then held her gaze more softly. 'What happened to you, Eva? Something has. You look awful.'

His tenderness was worse to bear than his growling. It made her want to melt down to being a little girl again when he could solve all her problems. But that wasn't why she was here. 'I've been working all summer on an island off South America. Researching tropical frogs.'

'Okay. And?'

'And I was good at it,' she shouted, 'okay?' Mimicking him.

'So this is what it's all about,' Jason said impatiently. 'Eva Martinez proving herself yet again.'

'What do you mean?' Eva's anger deflated. She pushed her hair off her face. Now it stuck up in frizzy curls just as wildly as her father's in the heat.

'Ever since your unfortunate incident as a student with that awful boy, you've fought to give two hundred percent to all that you do. I wonder whether you ever like what you do? Or is it all to prove yourself?'

She was taken aback. 'You and Gwendolin keep reminding me of the Connecticut incident. How I let you both down. I . . . I don't want to be that person. So yes, I do give everything all I've got.'

Jason sighed. Now he came fully into the room to sit on the chair opposite her. His long legs stretched out awkwardly. The chair wasn't designed for comfort. 'We should take some blame then. We should stop reminding you of it. It's just that your mother and I want you to succeed in life and to be happy.' It was an apology. Or as near one as her father could get. Which was okay by Eva.

There was a silence between them while she absorbed his words. Then she heard herself say, 'I met Bob Grierson.'

'So you know the truth then,' he replied evenly.

'I'm sorry about what I said. About you cheating on Gwendolin,' she said painfully. Yes, it was hard saying sorry but she had to do it.

He raised his eyebrows, acknowledging what she'd managed. 'It was a long time ago. I got over it. By the time it happened, your mother and I were already separating. When I met Nancy, it didn't matter to me anymore. But it did to you,' he finished gently.

'I wanted to blame you,' Eva

admitted. 'I was so angry for so long. But when I saw Gwendolin and Bob together this summer, it all fell into place.'

'Bob's good for her,' Jason said. 'He lets her win. He's a nice guy and he has no ego to stroke.'

'And you do?' Eva grinned.

'Yeah, you know that. My ego's so huge I've trouble getting in the door at dinnertime.' Jason was grinning too and suddenly it was all okay between them.

'I'm glad I came back here. I love this place,' she said. It was a gift to him.

He accepted it gladly. 'Nancy and I love having you. Stay as long as you want.' He hefted his case. 'Now, if you'll excuse me, I'll change into something cooler. Bring your old dad a beer, will you. Lots of ice.'

Eva looked out the window, seeing not the people hurrying by New York quickly, but herself young and naïve running after a scruffy youth who didn't care about her, and messing up in the process. Probably despite his almost-apology, her father would throw it at her again in future arguments. He couldn't help it. He used any ammo he could find. But it had lost the power to hurt her. Dan was right. She should please herself. Make herself happy. Jason had his own life here with Nancy. They were clearly still in love and had made a home together. Gwendolin was content, after a fashion, in her London house. Her on-off relationship with Bob suited her. So where did that leave Eva?

* * *

'I'll come with you,' Nancy offered. 'The hospital is a real rabbit warren. It'll take both of us to find the ward, I bet.'

Eva had tracked Dan down to the Beth Israel Medical Center in Manhattan. On the phone, the nurse she'd finally been passed to wouldn't tell her anything. 'I'm his partner,' Eva said when the nurse said only next of kin were being informed.

'Maybe you are, but you could be anyone over the line. If you wanna find out about him, you need to come visit.' She had at least provided the visiting hours for Eva.

Nancy hailed a yellow cab and it hurtled through the thick traffic towards the hospital and Dan. Eva's heart pounded. She couldn't wait to see him. He said he loved her and she knew she loved him too, now and forever. But Dan hadn't said what he wanted for them in the future. There hadn't been time before Sam burst in with his news of Rose's disappearance. So what did Dan think about them as a couple? She swallowed nervously and Nancy squeezed her hand in comfort, misreading her apprehension.

The hospital smelt like any other, antiseptic and bleach covering other less pleasant scents. There was a long line at reception and a woman at the front shouting at the person behind the desk. Finally the man next in line intervened, there was a light scuffle and the security guard steered them both along to a room. The door shut, and the queue shuffled along until it was Eva's turn.

They were sent up to a ward miles away, Nancy's high heels clicking like ticker-tape as they hurried. Eva was desperate, now she was so close. Her trainers squeaked on the linoleum in tandem with Nancy's clicks. She wore a light green dress. It was blessedly cool in the stifling heat.

'Dan Adams?' The nurse at the desk was bored and didn't bother to hide it. She took her time, lifting a register and turning a page with a wetted finger.

'Yes, he was airlifted here a few days ago from South America,' Eva said. She waited, her nerves screaming. She wanted to jump over the desk and grab the paperwork from the woman. There was a metallic taste in her mouth. She smelt the nurse's sweat and saw the dark stains of dampness under the armpits of her tight uniform. From somewhere the scent of roses, sickly sweet, made her almost gag. The air conditioning whirred, working over-time.

Then the nurse was shaking her head.

'What?' Eva said, too loudly.

The woman looked at her reproach-fully. 'You're too late.'

'Too late?' Eva echoed. Beside her, Nancy touched her shoulder in sup-port.

'Yeah, Mr Adams's injuries were less serious than first thought. His brother arrived this morning from the UK and took him home.'

He was gone! She'd left it too late and now she'd missed him entirely. She had no idea where he lived or where Tom lived. Then she froze. Dan hadn't asked for her. He couldn't have, or they'd have found her. Sent for her. The floor began to spin and nausea rose up in her throat. Eva pressed her hand to her mouth and ran for the toilets.

She threw up and threw up. She was vaguely aware of Nancy's voice. She staggered over to the sink to rinse her mouth. In the mirror she looked ghastly. Behind her Nancy looked concerned.

'It's this awful virus, nothing but fatigue and sickness. When will it stop?' She leaned on the sink.

'Are you sure it's a virus?' Nancy asked gently.

'What else could it be?'

15

Central Park was sharp with heat. The air simmered, the skyscrapers in the backdrop blurry. There were people everywhere in bright summer clothing enjoying New York's very own wilderness. A roller-blader clad in the skimpiest of shorts and a neon sling shirt whizzed by, curving round Eva at the last minute skilfully. Music blared, rap beat harsh, from outsized earphones. Eva headed for the lake. The pram was cumbersome and difficult to get round the curve in the path. She stumbled, hitting her shin on the metal bag net underneath, and cried out. The baby slept on. Eva steered the pram down the slope and parked it in the shade by the stone outcrop. A gang of young kids scrambled and climbed on the boulders, laughing and shouting. Their mothers, a group of four young women, sat beyond on a picnic blanket chatting and drinking from tall cups with straws. She felt a sudden pang of envy. They looked so happy and relaxed.

She checked that Lin was okay. Her little feet were bare and she lay on top of her wraps to keep her cool, dressed only in a blue checked cotton dress and diaper. The complicated parasol attached to the pram shaded her from the piercing sun. Jason had turned out to be a competent grandfather, capable of constructing all the paraphernalia of new parenthood. The lake glittered and she saw little boats on the opposite side.

'Oops. Sorry about that.' There was a grinding noise behind and she turned to find a young woman wearing an apologetic wince. Her baby pram had collided with Lin's.

'No damage done,' Eva said. She turned back to contemplating the lake.

But the woman was talking again. 'Hey, you're English, am I right? How do you like New York? How old's your little girl? Isn't she just a cutie?'

In London, no one would have talked to her. One of the things that Eva loved and hated about her home town. You could glide through London all day, touch a thousand people and yet speak to none of them. New York was different. Here she had random conversations with everyone, from the fishseller near Staten Island when she was waiting for a cab, to the owner of the shop where she bought a box of noodles one day, needing to catch a late lunch. It was the English accent that did it. The Americans couldn't resist it. They wanted to know her opinion on the USA and wanted her to love it. Inevitably they were slightly disappointed to learn that she'd lived half her life there on and off.

Nellie lived in the Bronx with her little girl Tiana, who was three months old, the same age as Lin. 'I love her to bits but it's tough. Broken nights, bottles of feed hour after hour. Man, I get fed up heating up milk. But look at her. She's adorable.'

'She's beautiful,' Eva agreed, truthfully. Tiana was a tiny copy of Nellie, with dark brown eyes and shiny, raven curls. She wriggled and smiled at her mother when Nellie playfully tickled her tummy.

'What about you? Finding it easy? Duck-to-water style?' Nellie asked, watching Eva adjust Lin's sun hat carefully.

She wanted to say yes to this stranger. Give it the lie. Yes, everything was perfect. She was a natural, instinctive mother and Lin was an easy baby. But when she opened her mouth, the truth spilled out instead.

'I don't think I'm cut out for this. I've got a baby book and I have to refer to it constantly. I thought I'd just know what to do but I don't. I'm scared I'll hurt her, drop her or she'll roll out of her pram. Is that natural?'

Nellie nodded. 'Totally. I was the same with my first. He's four now and playing at my mom's today but man, I was totally freaked by him when he was tiny. Are you getting any help?'

'My step-mother is helping but she doesn't have children so we're learning together.' She and Nancy both referred to the book when stumped. 'My mother's arrived to see her first grandchild so I can't complain about being on my own.' Gwendolin had flown in the day before. There was an uneasy truce between her and Jason, which was why Eva had escaped from the house to the park. Granny Gwendolin had plenty of ideas about how Eva should be raising her child.

'No partner, huh?' Nellie asked sympathetically, 'It's tough being a single mom. My guy was too ready with his fists. I took it but when he started in on the kids I threw him out. What about yours?'

'He wasn't violent, nothing like that,' Eva said, 'but he didn't want to know.' It hurt to say it but it wasn't the sharp agony of the previous year. It had dulled to a nagging ache which wouldn't heal.

Why had Dan not got in touch? He had cut Eva out of his life as cleanly as a blade slicing lemon. After she'd gone to the hospital with Nancy last year to find that Tom had taken Dan home, she'd phoned Bob Grierson and asked him to pass on a message to Dan. Her best wishes for his recovery. *Her love.* No, she'd kept that back, saying it silently. Her message was meant to tell him that she cared and that he should contact her. But he hadn't. And Eva's stubborn pride wouldn't let her humiliate herself again by seeking him out. If Dan Adams wanted to find her, it wasn't difficult. He could easily get Gwendolin's home address from Bob. Probably he thought Eva long back in London. He could've stepped up to the house and rung the bell. Okay, she was on the other side of the Atlantic Ocean; but if he made a move towards her, she and Lin would be back in London like a shot. He didn't even know he had a beautiful daughter.

'How could he not want to be a father to such a cute kid?' Nellie said.

Eva flushed. Nellie had misunderstood. It wasn't Lin that Dan had rejected. How could he when he didn't know of her existence? It was Eva who was hurt with his neglect. Eva who turned it over in her mind constantly, even twelve months after last seeing him. Why? Sometimes she blamed herself. Wasn't it her, after all, that had said originally it was only a holiday fling, a physical thing between them? Had it been that for him too? Had she imagined all his protestations of love? That last day in the tent before he went following off after Rose — she hadn't imagined that. Lin was proof it had happened. Nancy had turned out to be right about the sickness and although Eva's pregnancy had shocked her, she was delighted, too, to have Dan's baby. And always, after that trail of thought, fast stepping on its heels, was he still in love with Rose even after the awful events she'd wrought?

'Gotta go,' Nellie said, glancing at her watch, 'Gotta pick up TJ from my mom's. You take care of yourself, you hear me? Nice meeting you.'

Eva waved her goodbye. The young mothers had packed up their picnic and called their children down from the rocks. The boats were off the lake. Even the number of roller-bladers had dropped. She couldn't put it off much longer. She'd have to go home.

★   ★   ★

'You like that, you do? I can tell. Want me to do it some more?' Nancy laughed, leaning over a wriggling Lin on the changing mat. She tickled the baby's kicking toes and Lin gurgled happily. Eva felt a fierce love fill her. She couldn't imagine life without Lin now. There were no regrets. She was twenty-seven, a single mother and a million miles away from her ambition to have a research grant and work in

London. But it was okay.

'Yeah baby, Nana Nancy's here. Do you love her? Do you love your Nana?' Nancy chatted on in a crooning voice to Lin, who reached up with chubby hands and grabbed her long hair. Nancy kissed her on her button nose as she disentangled her sticky grasp. 'You need a bath, honey. Mommy's gonna run you one.'

'Mommy's right on the job,' Eva agreed, filling the baby bath up carefully and testing the temperature with her elbow the way Gwendolin had shown her. 'You're a natural with her, Nancy. Didn't you want any kids yourself?' Although the kids would've had Jason as a father, which might not have worked, Eva thought fleetingly, going by her own experience.

'Your Dad wanted more kids,' Nancy said, bringing Lin over to the bath and setting her gently into it, 'once we were together and knew it was forever. I got pregnant real quick. But I lost the baby eight weeks into it. It happened again and again. After the fifth, we stopped. We couldn't take it anymore. The joy, the hoping and praying and wishing. Then the sadness.'

'I didn't know.' Eva cradled Lin so her head was high of the water. 'I'm so sorry.'

Nancy smiled sadly down at Lin. 'Some things aren't meant to be, I guess. Now I get the chance to be a nana to this gorgeous girl. It was good of your mom.'

'She amazed me,' Eva said. 'First Lin gets to call her Granny — when I don't even get to call her Mum! Then she offers that you can be the other gran. Wow. I didn't see that coming. But it's great. She's softening in her old age.'

'You'd better not say that to her,' Nancy laughed. 'Gwendolin doesn't think she's getting old. But yeah, mellowing definitely. It was nice of you to name the baby after her. She sure melted at that.' They stole a glance at each other and grinned.

From downstairs came raised voices,

then a silence. Nancy sighed. 'I'd better get down there before they get stuck into each other. It's like grade school all over.'

'They've never been able to be in the same house for long,' Eva said. 'Lin's doing a grand job of bringing them together but they'll never change, will they.'

'I guess not, but don't you let them disturb you. You concentrate on Lin. She's the most important person in all this.'

Eva lifted the dripping and sweet-smelling baby from the shallow bath and laid her on a towel to dry. 'Yes, she is, isn't she. I love her to bits.'

Nancy hesitated at the door. She turned back to Eva. 'Don't you want to try again, honey? It wouldn't hurt to send a letter or phone him. He's got a right to know he's a father.'

Eva shook her head. 'He doesn't care. If he did, he'd have got in touch before now.'

Nancy sighed again. Downstairs,

Gwendolin's voice rose in a query. Nancy hurried down to keep the peace. Eva towelled Lin dry and sang her a song. But all she could think of was Dan. What was he doing right this minute? Did he ever think of her? Or had he moved on with his life, putting her in a box labelled 'holiday romance'? That seemed the most likely answer.

Dinner was an upmarket takeaway ordered in by Gwendolin. There was lamb curry and onion bhajis, two kinds of rice, fried spiced eggplant and tubs of chilli sauce. Eva took a sleepy Lin downstairs and lay her in her cot. She fixed the baby monitor so they could hear her in the dining room.

'Have you checked the batteries on the monitor?' Gwendolin asked.

'They're fine. I put new ones in yesterday.'

'Don't give me that look, darling. I'm only thinking of Lin's safety. Someone has to.'

'What does that mean? I'm constantly looking after her.'

'Yes and you're doing a grand job. I'm only saying ... ' Gwendolin soothed. She was distracted by the tubs of hot food and started dishing them out onto warmed plates on the dining table.

Jason sat at the head of the table and poured the wine. 'What your mother is trying to say is that Lin needs two parents. She needs a father. She needs *her* father.'

Gwendolin snapped the lid of the curry container loudly. 'That's not what I'm saying at all. Trust you to get the wrong end of the stick as usual. Eva doesn't need that man. She's better off without him. There's something dangerous about the fellow.'

Eva dropped the serving spoon in exasperation, the curry half-ladled. 'That's ridiculous, Mum, and you know it. Dan's not dangerous or odd or suspicious or any of the other things you've labelled him. You never gave him a chance. You never tried to get to know him. If you had, you'd have found out what a strong, trustworthy man he is. He's kind, he's clever — he's a doctor for goodness sake — he helps people. You should have seen him treating the team when someone got hurt. He was gentle and empathic.' She stopped, aware of three sets of eyes watching her. 'What?'

Nancy spoke first, gently. 'He sounds like a great guy, Eva, the way you tell it. There's a lot of emotion there. Your dad's right, you should try to contact him once more. Maybe he didn't get the message from Bob you sent. You owe it to Lin to try.'

'Now you're being ridiculous,' Gwendolin said to Nancy. 'I don't mean to be rude, but really, you've never met the man. It's perfectly possible to raise a child on one's own. Goodness, I managed it when Jason left me. Eva's doing the right thing. Dan Adams isn't interested. He's getting on with his own life and that's what Eva should be doing with hers. It was unfortunate that her holiday fling left her pregnant but it's not the end of the world. We're all here to help her, aren't we?'

'Why do you hate him so much?' Eva asked.

'I don't hate him, darling. But you have to admit it was all rather sudden, your sponsorship and running off to Trinita together. You didn't even invite me to the pre-expedition party to celebrate you all going. I had to gate-crash it. Your own mother. Imagine.'

Eva finally got it. Her mother was hurt. Underneath Gwendolin's cool and cultured veneer there was a softness she hadn't guessed at. All her life it felt as if her mother had kept her deliberately at arm's length. *Don't call me mother. Don't bother me darling, I'm working. Keep the noise down, Eva.* Gwendolin had been off-hand when Eva announced her intention to go to Trinita so suddenly. But she had turned up to the party. She had tried in her own way to be involved. No wonder she didn't like Dan. In her mind, he'd stolen her daughter.

'It's just like you to make a fuss, Gwen,' Jason commented, lifting his wine glass for a long sip. 'You've known about the expedition much longer than me. I was the last to know. Only found out when Eva came home last year.'

'This isn't about you,' Gwendolin said icily. 'Please don't bring everything back round to you. Besides, this isn't Eva's home. Her home is in London with me. In fact, I want to take Eva and Lin back with me when I fly home next week.'

As Gwendolin and Jason locked stares in battle, Nancy calmly laid down her cutlery and spoke directly to Eva.

'What do you want, honey? We all want what's best for you. Your Dad and I would love it if you and Lin stayed here with us. But your Mom clearly misses you. And Dan's in England — this could be your chance to find him. If not for yourself, then for Lin's sake.'

Later, Eva stood in her darkened

bedroom staring out of the window. Behind her she heard Lin's even breathing from the cot at the end of her bed. A mobile of butterflies and leaves hung over the cot. In the silhouette cast by the lamp from the hall, it looked like tangled jungle vines. Outside, the city was aglow with coloured lights from tall buildings and cars racing fast along the city streets. New York never slept. She had a decision to make. She could stay here with Jason and Nancy and make a life. Or she could go back to London with Gwendolin, who had even promised to look after Lin while Eva went back to work. She could chase that research contract she'd once longed for.

She had to make a decision about the rest of her life. But it wasn't simply about her and what she wanted anymore. It was about Lin. What was best for her. Would she blame Eva as she grew older for not letting her have the chance of knowing her father?

She pulled the curtains closed against the city and slipped under the duvet to lie, looking up at the ceiling. Could she swallow her pride and contact Dan? Her heart had already made the decision and Eva knew it wasn't because of Lin. It was her. She had to see him. Even if he had changed his mind and didn't love her and didn't want to know her. She would tell him she loved him. Find closure of some sort. Then go on with her life somehow. It would be weighted with lead but she'd find strength because of her daughter. Dan's daughter.

She rolled over, tucking the duvet round her as snug as a camping bag. Her dreams were of jungle creatures and fire and a man, a reassuring presence who hovered just beyond her reach.

16

Dan was helping Tom to build a double swing set in Tom's large Sussex garden. He dug with verve, enjoying the ache in his muscles, a sign of his strength and renewed energy. It was good to have a task to concentrate on which blocked out his thoughts. They tired him every day, a background buzz of 'what if's and questions he couldn't easily switch off. Marianne, Tom's wife, called encouragement on the construction, from the patio at the rear of the house where she played with the twins.

'How's the leg?' Tom asked, pausing with the screwdriver and the paper instruction manual.

'It's good. Physically I feel back to normal. You and Marianne can stop fussing over me,' Dan said, but he grinned at his brother to show he wasn't serious.

'And the flashbacks?'

'Not nearly so many.' Dan had suffered vivid nightmares after his accident, reliving the terrifying moment of his fall in intense detail over and over. It was only the care of his family that had brought him back to health.

'That woman deserves to boil in hell,' Tom said, hammering in a strut with fierce blows.

'You'll bend that,' Dan observed mildly. He went on digging.

'For a man who was almost murdered, you're very forgiving.'

'Rose is sick. I don't blame her or hate her.' Dan leaned on the spade handle. 'I feel incredibly sorry for her. She has everything — beauty, wealth and intelligence — but she's stricken with mental illness. It's a tragedy for her and for her father. So no, I don't hate her.'

Dan remembered Sam's description of Rose's father's blustering anger when he arrived to collect her from the South American hospital. She was to be transferred to a private sanatorium. He was ready to lash out at Sam and anyone else involved, sure that it wasn't Rose's fault whatever had happened. The man had crumbled when Sam explained she'd tried to kill Dan. He'd then shaken Sam's hand in gratitude on learning there would be no police involvement. Dan had no intention of telling the world the events of that terrible day. All he wanted was for Rose to get treatment, Sam told him.

Besides, Dan's own memory of what had occurred was blurred. He had a head injury. Had she really stepped aside consciously to make him fall? Or was it an accident? So he played it when Sam or Bob asked him. There was no case to make. Rose and her father departed. Dan was already in the hospital in New York. Already replaying every minute of the tragedy until the nurse gave him another injection and blessed sleep infused him.

'You'd have recovered a lot quicker if you'd taken my advice and stopped work for a few months.' Tom frowned. The swing set lay ready for setting into the holes in the lawn that Dan had dug, but Tom had two screws left over. They lay on his open palm like a tiny puzzle.

'Work kept me sane. You should understand that, being a workaholic yourself. If I work, I don't think about Rose and Lunara Gorge. Simple as that.' Dan took the two screws from his brother and fitted them into the cross-strut.

'There's more though, isn't there? Things you're not saying. It's unlike you to keep secrets from me. We've always been close. I thought it was the fall and you didn't want to talk about it, but lately I've been thinking it's more than that. In the hospital, you kept calling out in your sleep. A girl's name. Who is she?'

The swing set was upright and set in place before Dan answered. Personally, he was ready to mix the cement and carry right on, but Tom had stopped determinedly, waiting for Dan to answer.

'The woman I love.'

'You what? When . . . '

'Last year. I fell in love with her in Trinita.'

'You never told me.' Tom sounded hurt.

'I couldn't, Tom. I'm sorry, but try to understand. I lost her. After the accident, she vanished from my life. Didn't want to know me.'

Tom nodded. 'You kept calling her name. The nurses were concerned; they asked me who she was and I couldn't help. When you were recuperating, it didn't seem right to ask you. I worried it would set your recovery back if I forced you to remember. Then with Mum's illness this year, there was never time to discuss it.'

'I fell in love with Eva.' There was a joy in saying her name. 'I thought she returned it but then it turned out I was wrong.'

'Are you certain?' Marianne had

listened in. The twins crawled nearby on the dry grass.

'When I got out of hospital and Tom brought me back here, I got in touch with Bob and he gave me Eva's address. I sent her a letter.' It had been a hard letter to write. He'd wasted several sheets of paper getting it right. In the end, he'd kept it simple. Told the truth. That he loved her. That he wanted to marry her. For her to please get in touch. He'd written Tom and Marianne's address at the bottom.

'And?' Marianne asked.

'And the letter was returned. No note, nothing. So I plucked up the courage to phone. She wouldn't listen. Put the receiver down.'

'Did she say anything? Did she say she didn't love you?' Marianne said.

'I did the talking,' Dan said. 'Rushed into my prepared speech. At the end, I waited to hear her answer. There was a click and then the disconnected signal. That was it. Stark and brutal perhaps, but it gave me my answer. She'd changed her mind about me. She didn't love me after all.'

Marianne grabbed one of the babies, who was about to eat a clump of grass. Dan swung his niece up in the air before she could miss her twin. She laughed and punched him on the nose with a tiny fist, making his eyes water. That was good. It disguised the emotional punch that talking about Eva brought on.

He'd sworn to let it go. Persuaded himself that he didn't feel deeply in love with her. It would do him no good to pine after her, a one-sided love affair. But it hadn't stopped the pain of missing her.

'The thing is,' Tom said slowly, 'you don't actually know that Eva received your letter or was the person who answered the telephone. Do you?'

Dan stared at him. 'I assumed she did. Why would someone else return my letter or put the phone down on me?' He put his niece slowly down on the lawn, where she crawled to her mother to be lifted. 'Even if for some reason it wasn't Eva, why hasn't she been in touch with me?'

'Perhaps life got in the way for her too,' Tom suggested. 'Don't you think you owe it to yourself to try one more time? If you really love her.'

'No.' Dan shook his head. 'It's over. She once told me it was a holiday romance, nothing more. It was a magical few weeks last summer, where we got caught up in the heat and passion of the adventure. I need to move on with my life now that I'm fit.'

'But Dan, this isn't like you. Where's the man whose confidence bulldozes everything in front of him?' Marianne teased gently. 'I can't believe you haven't gone looking for her. Never mind letters and phone calls, turn up on her doorstep. You know you can persuade the sun to come out on a cloudy day if you try!'

Dan held up his hand. 'Please, don't mention her again.'

* * *

But Dan couldn't forbid himself to mention Eva any more than he could force his body to stop eating. He was reminded of her when the temperature soared and an Indian summer beckoned. He remembered her delight in the exotic fruits in Trinita when he got back to London and shopped at a local market. The sparkle in her eye and her thirst for adventure. His body stirred when he thought of their passionate and tender lovemaking in the tent. He had fallen in love with her. She'd said she loved him too. But maybe it was the emotion of the moment that made her say it. There was no other explanation for her refusal to get in touch with him. If that was the way she felt, he had no right to pester her.

Marianne's words came back to him. Yes, the old Dan brushed all in his path aside with a monumental confidence — an arrogance, if he was truthful. It had served him well all his life. He was a natural leader. And confidence was essential in a doctor. Patients demanded it, needed it. But now . . . his love for Eva had left him uncertain. If he delved deeper into his psyche, he knew that what had happened with Rose had changed him too. His confidence in his ability to judge character had been shaken to the core. He'd wanted to marry Rose. And she ended up almost killing him. Was he wrong about Eva too? Had he imagined the delight in her eyes when she saw him?

He might have stayed in limbo longer if he hadn't had a call from his partner at the London practice. Tom had driven him back to London after the long weekend and Dan was preparing for work the next day when Mike phoned.

'How's it going, mate?' Mike's rich Australian accent was upbeat as usual. Nothing got Mike down; he was one of life's optimists.

'Is there a problem?' Dan was immediately on alert. He and Mike ran the doctors' surgery with two other permanent staff and a locum. Mike was senior partner, a deliberate decision on Dan's part which allowed him to take extended leave and join expeditions abroad every year.

'No probs. I'm phoning to tell you your holidays have arrived early. Three weeks of them, to be precise.'

'What are you on about, Mike? I haven't got time to take any holidays.'

'I've got a locum in to cover you,' Mike went on blithely. 'Go somewhere nice, drink some beers and chase some girls. Whatever does it for you. But come back relaxed and focused. Okay?'

Dan could hardly refuse. He knew he'd been distracted lately but thought he'd covered it well. Clearly he hadn't. Mike was cheerful but his message was blunt: get himself sorted or stay away until he was.

He wandered around the house aimlessly, his work shirt and tie dropped on the bed and his medical bag sitting open. Three weeks off. What would he do? He hung the shirt back on a hanger in the wardrobe and put the tie on the special tie rack that Tom and Marianne had bought him the previous Christmas. It was a joke present but was useful in its way. He went to shut his bag and instead knocked it over. The contents spilled out onto the floor. With a curse, he knelt to pick them up.

A photograph had fallen from the inside slip pocket. He picked it up. It was the team shot from Trinita, taken in front of the tents on the first day after they'd arrived. There were James and Christa grinning into the camera lens, arms linked; Sam and Daisy; Bob, looking like the mad boffin with his white aura of hair; the divers, with Gail the only unsmiling face in the crowd. And Eva, smiling to camera, looking slender and beautiful with her wild black hair under the red bandanna. Would he be the only one to detect vulnerability, even nervousness in her face? She was a mix of pride and determination and fragility. Dan's heart swelled until it felt like it filled his entire chest. The photograph dropped leaf-like from his grasp and floated zigzag to the floor.

17

John. F. Kennedy airport was as busy and sticky with heat as he remembered from previous trips to New York. He hailed a taxi outside the airport building with difficulty, and then he was speeding along in a yolk-coloured car following the arteries of the city to its very heart. He took out the address again and Gwendolin's spiky lettering describing exactly where the brownstone was.

She'd been extremely surprised to see him. She couldn't hide her shock but politely invited him in when it became clear he wouldn't budge from her doorstep until she did.

He went straight to it, a bite to the jugular because he'd run out of time. 'It was you that day on the phone, wasn't it? Listening to me pour out my soul and making the decision to cut me off. I daresay you intercepted my letter to Eva too. Where is she, Gwendolin? Where is she?'

'She isn't here.' Gwendolin's cut-glass accent was pure ice.

'What's next? Are you going to tell me that you'll never tell me where she is, that I'll never find her?' he mocked, his own anger cold as frozen metal.

She didn't say anything for a moment, then indicated that he should follow her along the hall. He did so until they stood in a beautifully furnished room, full of antiques and expensive oil paintings. He was unimpressed. If Gwendolin hoped to intimidate him with the surroundings, she'd be disappointed. But he had misjudged her. She sank down onto a spindly chair which wouldn't have looked out of place in an ancestral castle.

'You really do love her, don't you?'

'Don't doubt it,' he said, the metal hard and unyielding. 'I'm in love with Eva and I won't stop until I find her and tell her.'

The air left Gwendolin's lungs in a rush. She suddenly looked smaller and less confident. 'Yes, it was me that listened to your call. I got the letter and I opened it. I . . . I didn't want Eva to get hurt. All that business with the girl Rose. I couldn't be sure you were good for her. That rushed sponsorship, the whole escape to Trinita. You can understand that, can't you?'

'Except it wasn't your call to make.'

'No, no, you're right. But you're not the only one who loves Eva.' Some spirit was left in her voice as she raised her head to stare at him.

'I can assure you that I'm the only one who is *in* love with her,' Dan said, 'with a passion and promise enough for a lifetime and beyond. So tell me where she is, please.'

Her next words were burned in his memory forever.

'She's in New York at her father's house. She's living there with your daughter. I've just visited them.'

* * *

The woman who opened the door was pretty, with blonde hair and a neat physique. He was ready with an introduction but she beat him to it, treating him to a warm smile when she spoke. 'It's Dan, isn't it? You finally made it. She's out in the park for a walk. Do you want to wait here for her?'

Central Park was full of New Yorkers making the most of a hot summer Saturday and an array of tourists getting lost in the vast wild areas or eating ice-cream from the vendors on the tarmac nearer town. Nancy had described the place where Eva liked to go, a quiet spot on the edge of the lake.

She had her back to him, staring out at the glittery surface of the water where sailboats sped past. She was even more slender than he remembered, but her hair was just as wildly curly. Beside her was a pram. He couldn't see the occupant but his heart lurched in a mixture of emotions. He was a father!

He stopped dead on the path. This was a moment, suspended in a precious drop, before everything changed. He savoured her from the distance. His love, his life, his future.

'Eva?' His voice cracked on her name.

She spun round, her mouth a round circle of surprise. Then she stood, simply staring at him. He moved towards her. She moved a little too but not enough to make the embrace he sought. Her hand went protectively to the handle of the pram.

'Why didn't you tell me?' Dan gestured at the pram. Still, he couldn't see the baby. *His baby*.

'Is that why you came? For Lin?' Eva said sadly. She pushed the pram round so he could see in.

Dan looked in to see a perfect little girl with Eva's big grey eyes and a head of curly black hair. She had his warm colouring. She gave him a gummy smile.

'She's wonderful,' he said softly. He

looked up at Eva, wanting them to agree on this, their very own miracle.

She frowned darkly at him. 'What do you want from me? Is it access to Lin? Did Gwendolin let my little secret out then?'

'I came for you,' he said.

Her face softened at that but she still held herself prickly like an offended cat. 'I sent you a message via Bob. After you left the hospital and your brother took you back to England. You never replied.'

'I never got it,' Dan said. He could guess who had. He imagined Bob telling Gwendolin about Eva's message and being persuaded by the woman he loved to leave it, not to stir what was best left alone. 'I wrote to you and tried to contact you. Don't blame your mother, she did what she thought was right.'

Eva clenched her fists and turned away to look back out at the lake. In the pram, Lin started to cry. Instinctively they both went to her, their hands touching as they comforted their child. She waved her little arms at them, her eyelids drooped and she fell asleep.

'Eva,' Dan whispered, his throat dry, 'I came to tell you that I love you and that I can't live without you. Will you marry me?'

'Isn't this about Lin? About you doing the right thing and stepping up to the mark of being a father?'

'No.' He reached for her and she didn't pull away. 'It's about us. I want you and I need you.'

Then she sagged against him and whispered, 'I love you too. I've missed you so much. I never thought you'd come back to me. That Rose was right, that I'd wait in vain. I was getting ready to go back to London to find you. My mother was begging me to go back with her but I couldn't. I had this feeling, an instinct, that I had to wait here.'

Dan kissed her firmly on the lips, pressing on them until she kissed him back. Her lips were soft and warm and enticing and he parted them urgently with a seeking tongue and a rising heat. He pulled her body to him until they were moulded as one with desire flaming between them. He wanted her right there. Was desperate for her like a thirsty man for water. Now she was holding him tightly, fiercely, hands locked behind his head while she kissed him. She couldn't get any closer to him without melting right into his flesh. With a ragged breath, she drew back.

'I will marry you,' she said with a laugh redolent with happiness.

Dan bent his head and kissed her again.

Epilogue

Eva shivered in her cream velvet dress. London in late September was chilly, the country preparing for a cold, damp English autumn now that the promise of the Indian summer had evaporated. Gwendolin had insisted on the marquee in the garden. Luckily it was attached to the back door of the house, so at least the guests could move between the two without going outside.

'Cold, my love?' Dan was there with her matching cream shawl, which he expertly draped around her shoulders. In his other arm, he held their daughter. Lin was dressed in a strawberry-pink dress and matching shorts for her parents' wedding reception.

Gwendolin had offered to host it at her London home and Jason and Nancy had flown over for the celebrations. Angelica, too, had made the journey, all the way from Trinita. Eva was nervous about meeting Dan's parents but she needn't have worried. They were lovely and took to her and Lin instantly. Lin was the lucky grandchild of three grandmothers, all keen to spoil her and dote on her; and lucky, too, to have a great-grandmother equally delighted in her. Tom and Marianne and Lin's twin cousins were there too. Eva and Marianne had struck up a friendly conversation about their children and she had a feeling that Dan's sister-in-law would turn out to be a great friend.

'The climate's a bit different from Trinita,' Dan said, kissing her cheek. Lin tugged at her Daddy's nose until he kissed her too.

'I think I've had enough of the tropics to last me a while,' Eva said. 'I'm perfectly content to settle here in the cold in my favourite city with my favourite husband and child.'

Jason, walking past, paused.

'With frequent visits to my other

favourite city, of course,' Eva said, grinning at him. 'Lin would miss her grandpapa and nana otherwise.'

Dan cuddled her close until she and Lin were wrapped in his embrace. 'Wherever we are, it's home when we're together,' he told her.

Eva kissed her husband and knew that he was right.